SPOUT
WATER
THE
UP

DORIS MUSICK

Wishing you joy!
Doris Musick

ISBN: 978-1-891029-25-7 (Paper)
ISBN: 978-1-891029-23-3 (Hardbound)

Up the Water Spout

Copyright 2006 by Doris C. Musick

This book has been printed and bound in the United States of America. All rights reserved. No part of this book may be reproduced in any form or by electronic or mechanical means without the expressed consent of Doris Musick, Author.

The cover, '*Rail Road Depot, Abingdon, VA*' was painted in water color by the late Roma Baker and is used with the consent of her husband, Leon Baker. The above stipulations regarding reproductions also apply.

First Edition.

Up the Water Spout is a work of fiction. The places and dates are real, but the characters are fictional. Many of the scenes have been taken from stories told to the author over a period of years, but should not be tied to any specific persons in the area, whether living or dead.

HENDERSON PUBLISHING
811 Eva's Walk, Pounding Mill, VA 24637

Special Thanks

To Katie, Michael, and especially to Larry

Appreciation to Karen, Tim & Mark
And to the grandchildren,
Brandon & Dylan

IN MEMORY
Roma

Roma Wilson Baker
1934 – 1998

A life long resident of Washington County, Virginia, Roma nonetheless had traveled abroad many times in search of inspiration for her paintings, covering some nine countries in this pursuit. However, nothing inspired her as much as her own 'turf' as she painted numerous realistic and charming scenes from the Abingdon area. She felt many of these old landmarks would fade in time, but once captured on canvas they were ours to enjoy forever. Copies of her numbered prints abound.

On a personal side, she gained much pleasure from painting Victorian scenes; a quaint day in a white gazebo with a cup of tea served on a lace tablecloth, or ladies in broad brimmed white hats with flowing ribbons. These scenes spoke of the real Roma, the quiet spoken lady who appreciated the niceties of a home on a quiet street, of sharing brunch with a friend, of leisurely walks at the pond while the ducks swam quietly about...............

An unassuming and gracious person, my sister and my friend; Roma, we miss you.

CHAPTER 1

Greene County, Tennessee
1918

Steven was seven years old when Papa died.

The last day and a half as Papa lay in his casket in the parlor was like a bad dream. The neighbors came in their Model T Ford's, in wagons and on foot. Some of the men had stayed on through the night, sitting quietly in the room with Papa. Steven was glad. He didn't want Papa to be alone. Steven buried his face in his pillow on that night and tried to swallow the tears. Then he heard his brothers sniffing and he knew it was all right to cry.

Momma's friends came, bringing food. They would hug Momma gently, her tiny frame seeming to be so fragile she might break. "I'm so sorry, Rachael," they would say. "Edward was a fine man."

She was a proud woman and pulled herself up to her full five feet four inch height and pushed a wisp of long brown hair from her face. She prepared her hair into a bun, the style of the day, but the natural curl fought against the pins that would hold it in place. As the friends and neighbors greeted her, everyone would cry. Momma cried hardest of all, her beautiful blue eyes swollen and red from the hours of mourning. The visitors would turn and look mournfully at the children, pat Momma's shoulder, sniff a few tears and then move on to talk in hushed voices with other folks who had gathered.

"Poor Rachael," Steven would hear them say of his mother. "Whatever will she do now? And the poor thing looking peaked herself."

Sometimes they would hug him as they passed by, and Steven could smell the mixture of their lavender and sweat. He didn't like their hugs and tried to stay out of the way.

The food so thoughtfully provided was piled on the large oak table in the dining room. This room was usually put to use only on

1

very special occasions like Thanksgiving or Christmas, but now it was filled with *women*. They stood around talking and pretending not to eat but all the while filling their already laden plates. The men moved out to the front lawn where they could smoke or spit their tobacco.

A curious bee flew through the open door, perhaps with thoughts of sampling one of the pies. Steven shooed the uninvited visitor away as he stood gazing at the table. That sweet potato pie looked awfully tempting. It was his favorite. And he was so hungry. The last days before Papa died had not offered much in the way of eats. Momma had been busy caring for Papa and all his sister Susan knew how to cook was a choice of beans or potatoes with hard bread. No comparison to this wonderful looking pie. Steven could almost smell the sweet brown sugar he knew went into it's making.

"Why don't we move outside for a breath of fresh air?" one of the heavyset ladies asked. Steven found himself momentarily alone with the pie before him.   Absent of the female maze that had separated him from this treasure, he summoned his courage and bravely reached out for the biggest slice. Ignoring the plates or saucers, he carried the tasty morsel in his hands.

Steven made a hasty retreat out the back door, and circling the house toward the front he stopped at the side and crawled through the broken lattice work. He inched his way under the porch. He had many times followed the family dog through this same opening, but today ole Fritz was tied out back due to all the extra folks being around. And so Steven found the one place where he could eat his delicacy in peace.

It filled the emptiness in his stomach while he simultaneously experienced a feeling of guilt for its pleasure under such circumstances. It would forever leave him with a mixed feeling of joy and sadness whenever he devoured a special treat. At especially sad times in his life he could imagine he was inhaling the clean smell of the earth as he was experiencing it now, safely hidden under the porch floor.

"Steven."   It was his Aunt Martha calling to him.   "Where are you?"

2

Aunt Martha wasn't truly a relative, but being his mother's best friend he always addressed her as such. He wanted so to stay under the porch, but Aunt Martha was a kind person, and he didn't have the heart to hide from her. He slowly climbed out through the lattice opening.

"Come along," she said softly, "it's time for you boys to get your shoes on, and I want you to put on your very best pair of trousers."

"Yes'm." Steven replied meekly. He knew it was time to take Papa away.

Steven shared a room with his brothers on the second floor and for once was glad for their company. He was also glad he wasn't the oldest. His uncles from Virginia had taken his two older brothers, Harold and Randolph, aside and lectured them on their responsibility now that Papa had died. His only sister, Susan, had already assumed much of the housework and so was not chastised, or at least not yet. Steven was glad he was fourth in line. Not much would be expected of a seven year old, except to look after the two younger boys. Will at five years old wasn't going to be a problem; he and Will had always been close and played together well. Steven wasn't as sure about handling the younger Rodney, but knew Will would help him.

"Stevie, those socks don't match." It was Harold who was pointing out Steven's miss-matched socks and grudgingly helped him find its mate. Harold tried to run a comb through Steven's unmanageable crop of brown hair, and was less than pleased with the result. Will, quietly and in his own fashion, found his best pair of long trousers, albeit they only came to his ankles, and put them on and after tying his shoes stood silently waiting for the others. Randolph was helping Rodney with his shoes and from this confusion the boys emerged, ready for what lay ahead.

Together with their sister, they piled into Papa's old car for the ride to the Mount Zion Baptist Church, set among the marble stones. Harold had taken over as their main driver after Papa fell sick. Rachael rode in the fancy car just ahead of them with her two brothers from Virginia, Mason and Basil White. Basil had driven

3

his own car down to Greeneville and enjoyed showing it off. Momma had explained that Basil had made a trip all the way to London, England before the war started. He saw a fancy car called a "Benz" and had it shipped back home. It was the fanciest car in Abingdon, the small town where he lived in Virginia.

Steven wasn't sure how he felt about his uncles. At seven, he didn't always understand grownups. He had sensed his Papa's strong reserve whenever they came calling, which fortunately wasn't very often.

"Papa says they want to be called aristocrats." Harold had explained earlier.

"What is one?" Steven had asked, puzzled. He avoided trying to pronounce the big word.

"Best I can figure out, it's somebody who thinks they are better than everybody else." Harold replied solemnly. There was no malice in his voice, just conviction that he had hit upon the truth. Steven was pretty sure he was right, the uncles did have a bad habit of making people around them feel like they weren't quite as good.

Steven rode to his father's funeral in silence. He tried to study on different things and not think about what was going to happen next. He tried to recall his Papa teaching him to fish, and how important his Papa looked when he was standing behind the counter of his very own General Store. Steven liked going into his Papa's store with all the good smells, the pickle barrel, the cracker barrel, and on a good day, the peppermint sticks.

Papa had owned two stores in all, the one near their house being the largest. His Papa worked hard and kept long hours, and he had prospered. Steven didn't understand some of the big words he heard, but there was one word – *tuberculosis* — that came into their lives and nothing would ever be the same again.   Papa had to go away.   They called the place a sanitarium, a special hospital for people with an illness like Papa's. Momma tried to run the stores with the help of a manager, Bob Watson.   Within the first year, Momma found out he was stealing from the till and from the shelves. She didn't know what to do, so she sent Papa a letter. Papa was home in ten days. In twenty months and three days, Papa was dead.

4

Steven was jolted back to the present as the automobile stopped and the children climbed out. Harold, as the oldest, took charge and ushered all of them into the church and into the pew just behind their mother. Steven looked around. There were many faces he didn't know, they must be relatives who had traveled from a long distance, he thought. The Pastor began to speak.

"Heavenly Father, we are gathered here today to say goodbye to Your servant, Edward Williams.............."

Steven heard his mother crying softly into her handkerchief. He leaned forward and bent his head low. He allowed the tears to flow off his cheeks and splatter softly on the wooden floor of the Mount Zion Baptist Church.

CHAPTER 2

The drive home from the cemetery was silent. No one wanted to talk as the impact of Papa's death was beginning to settle over them. Steven looked at Harold, his head bent just a bit forward and his hands gripping the steering wheel tightly. Papa had taught Harold to drive. Who would teach him?

Their uncle's car was already in the driveway ahead and their mother was waiting. As Harold pulled the car in front of the house, she ran to embrace each child. She tried to smile and give assurance they were going to be all right.

" Papa wanted his family to remember the good times," she told them.

They walked toward the house, silently, pressing together as if their oneness could make the sadness go away. From the doorway, Steven could see the coat rack down the hall. His Papa's hat was still hanging there, a hat that would never be worn again. The finality of it caused a funny feeling in Steven's stomach. It was as if there was a big hole there and nothing was going to fill the emptiness. Steven saw that his uncles were making their departure so he remained where he was standing as his mother said her goodbyes to them. He didn't really mind their going, but he knew how he would feel if his own brothers were leaving, and so he did his best to mind his manners for his mother's sake.

Harold stood over to the side, not taking part in the farewells. He stood as straight as his fifteen year old frame would allow. He was the man of the house now. He knew he could never take his Papa's place, but he was the eldest. Randolph was only ten, and while he shadowed Harold's every step, Harold knew it would become his own duty to shoulder the burden of the family. And he was afraid.

"Take care of things, son" the uncles called to Harold. He didn't know why, but somehow their words rang out as a challenge.

Susan had gone into the house to assist Aunt Martha. At thirteen, Susan too was afraid. She had so adored her Papa and had grieved silently as she watched her mother nursing him futilely. They couldn't save Papa. What would happen to them now?

While Susan had tried to suppress her grief, Steven often saw her cry when she thought no one was around. He didn't always understand her tears. His only explanation was that girls do funny things. He had first resented Susan when she began to give him orders. "Wipe your feet.....wash your hands..." and the like. But then he noticed Susan wasn't the same Susan as before. She was more serious, not laughing and being a silly ole girl. She no longer took the time away from Momma and Papa to go for long walks after church, or go wading in the creek with the other girls. Even that boy she used to be sweet on didn't come around anymore. Harold and Randolph used to call him her pimply-faced sweetheart and Susan would get really mad. But now Steven saw that the boy would go walking with one of the other girls. When Susan saw them for the first time, she ran to her room to cry. Steven didn't understand that at all. Why would Susan care whom that dumb ole boy walked with? Steven didn't comprehend but he came to love his sister even more because somewhere in his young heart he knew she was doing all of this for him and for his brothers.

The neighbors were beginning to leave after expressing their last condolences. After a while, the family found themselves alone. Momma gathered all of them in the living room and began to talk, recalling many precious memories.

"Do you remember when your Papa took us all to the Fair and he and Harold chased the greased pig?" she asked them.

That brought smiles to the faces of the older children and a full reenactment of the scene for those too young to have been a part of that day. The spell had been broken and now each in turn told of a happy event they recalled. They had their memories. That was all they could cling to now. Steven felt especially bad for Will and Rodney. Will had not known his father during most of the good years, before Papa got sick. And Rodney being only three was hardly going to remember Papa at all. Sadness overcame Steven once again.

The days of summer slowly dragged by as the Williams family tried to cope with their loss. Horace Hilton, the Superintendent of Schools for Greene County wrote a note to Mrs. Rachael Williams and asked if he might meet with her in his office. This perplexed Rachael a bit, she wondered if any of the children had caused a problem. They all swore their innocence.

On the day of their meeting, Horace peered at her over his reading glasses worn balanced on the end of his nose. He would make her an offer which would solve many of their problems but pose another. He wanted to hire her to teach in the two room school, the one near their home and the same school her children had been attending for years.

The offer should not have been that surprising, both Rachael and Edward were educated people. Rachael's own credentials included being an honor student, graduated from a fine Virginia women's institution. But since her marriage and with her children to care for, she had never thought of returning to teaching.

"The suggestion would certainly be an answer to many of my concerns, but I know that the two teachers you currently employ have been with you for many years. I'm wondering why this sudden offer?"

"Well, ahemmm, it seems Mrs. O'Donnell has found herself in the family way……" he started, but seemed to be having a bit of trouble finding the right words.

"That is wonderful news. I know she and her husband must be delighted. They had just about given up." Rachael replied, enthusiastically.

"Yes, yes, I'm sure. But the dilemma I find myself in, with only two weeks until the beginning of the school term, I'm in need of a teacher. Can't let Mrs. O'Donnell continue you know. Not with her in a delicate way. We ask that she step aside during this time. We have always had this policy in effect here in Greene County." Horace explained to her.

"Yes, I do recall that now. I hadn't thought on it."

"Then you'll take the job? I'll have to tell you, Rachael, you are the only qualified teacher I have in the vicinity right now, and

9

you'd be helping us out here."

"And you would be helping me too, Horace. But I will have to think on it. You see, one of my children, Rodney, is only three and I'm not sure how I could provide for him on a day to day basis. Will is five and half and is a very bright boy. He is quiet, but is very smart. I could start him in first grade, I'm sure he would be just fine. And of course the other children would be in school too. But Rodney......... I just don't know. I'll have to work out something and let you know."

As fate would have it, Mason and Basil White returned to Greeneville that same weekend. They were pressuring Rachael to sell out. She resisted that plan and now could tell them about her teaching position. They thought they had the perfect solution to that problem. Their solution would lead to many months of grief and tears for Rachael.

"Horace," Rachael began when she again visited the Greene County School Board office, "I will accept the teaching position. My brothers have made arrangements for my youngest, Rodney, to live with relatives in Virginia temporarily."

"That's fine, fine. I'm so glad to hear it." Horace was beaming at her, obviously relieved at the outcome. "I know you will do a quality job for us."

"Yes, I will do my best." Rachael replied, not revealing the heartache and the nights she had cried herself to sleep seeing little Rodney taken from her to live with a family chosen by her brother Mason. She had grieved not knowing how long it might be before she could reclaim him.

"Just one thing, Rachael. If you have any evidence or even suspect you may have contracted the same disease as your husband, you must inform me at once," he asked.

"I wouldn't think of doing otherwise." Rachael had replied defiantly and had signed the teaching contract.

On the first day of school Steven climbed into the car with all his siblings, except for little Rodney, and they headed for the clapboard two room building which had schooled all the area residents of rural Greene County for many years. Harold drove as usual, with

Rachael riding up front balancing Will on her knees watching to be sure his dangling legs did not interfere with the floor's gear shift. Susan, Randolph and Steven filled the back seat.

The school building consisted of two very large rooms, separated by a roll up door between. On one side, classes were held for the sixth, seventh and eighth grades. A local spinster, Mae Webster, would be teaching this older group. Eighth grade level was as far as the local schools could carry students, beyond that they would have to go to one of the local boarding schools. Only the more affluent families could send their children for higher learning. The adjoining side of the school building was grades one through five. This would be Steven's classroom. It would be Rachael's classroom too.

On reaching the school, Harold and Susan hurried into their own class This would be Harold's last year at the little school. He would have completed the courses sooner but he had to take off the last two years when Papa was so sick, so he was returning to finish his last term. Even though his sister would be in the same grade level, he didn't mind. He had looked forward to returning with anticipation. But he didn't feel good about arriving at school with his mother! Perhaps the other students had seen him driving the family vehicle. That should prove how grownup he was.

Will had yearned to come to school. He had been so excited he couldn't sleep, awaiting his first day. Now, seeing all the confusion around him, he was suddenly afraid. He grabbed hold of Randolph's hand.

"Where will my desk be?" he asked with a tremble in his voice.

"Momma will tell us in a minute. Usually they separate all the grades."

This frightened Will even more as he feared being separated from his brothers. He held on to Randolph's hand even tighter.

"Don't worry, Will. You might be seated in a different row, but both Steven and me will be right in the same room with you. Besides, Momma is our teacher," his older brother reassured him.

"Hey, Randolph," called out Luke McVey. "Your Momma got a paddle?"

11

"You'll find out soon enough," replied Randolph.

"Aw, don't pay him no mind." Steven tried to be encouraging but the truth was he felt a little self-conscious too. He didn't think things were going to go too well for him. Seeing the teasing already starting, he dreaded recess.

"Huh! Guess we know who'll be teacher's pet," chided some of the boys.

"Probably won't have to do their homework either," said others.

"What's homework?" asked Will. This brought on laughter from the girls who had been standing around, but not entering into the joshing.

"Take your seats, children." Rachael commanded in her most pleasant but no-nonsense voice. "First grade, please be seated in row one," she requested.

Randolph pried Will's hand loose from his own and led him to one of the smaller desks. There was the noise of scraping chair legs against the wooden floor as the older siblings tried to help with the younger ones, new to how the multi-grade system would be set up. Soon the desks were arranged in rows of smallest to largest with each row of desks representing a different grade level.

The weeks of autumn flew by as Rachael tried to ease into her new routine. Each of the family had taken on some new level of responsibility. These roles were not directed but rather a matter of necessity. Will had taken charge of the dog, Fritz, without being reminded or relying on one of the older boys. Susan was learning to be a much better cook, sometimes as good as her mother. Harold and Randolph took care of the heavier jobs like pushing the old mower through the yard once a week as they had had to do all summer, and now they raked leaves and helped dig potatoes. Steven had learned how to wring a chicken's neck and pluck all the feathers. He didn't like the job, but he sure did like fried chicken on a Sunday!

For Rachael, Saturday was filled with catching up on the housework and those mounds of dirty clothes. It was on these days at home that she missed Rodney most as she would take out her frustrations and fears on the washboard. Edward had planned to have electricity run to the house but then he had fallen ill and those things had to wait. Rachael could certainly have used one of those new-fangled washing machines she had seen in the Sears and Roebuck catalog. But no matter how hard she tried to push the sadness aside, her thoughts kept coming back to her baby boy. So many times she wished she had fought her brother Mason a bit harder when he suggested this solution for Rodney.

"Sister, you are being foolish," he had told her. "You can't keep all of the children here and the Miners are one of the most respected families in Damascus." Mason had not expected her hesitation to his plan. He was not accustomed to his decisions being challenged.

"But he is such a little thing. How do you know they will treat him kindly?" she argued.

"You are being foolish. Besides, Damascus is only a short drive from my home in Abingdon. I'm sure I'll see Rodney often. They are not mean people. Why, Dr. Miner is an educated man."

"Edward always called him a 'quack,' not a doctor." Rachael retorted.

"That's absurd. There's nothing wrong with James, that is, Dr. Miner. He's a friend. His wife can't have any more children except that one...... that one..., er, what the devil is her name?" Mason blustered.

"Her name is Abigail and she is slow-witted. There was a problem at birth," Rachael explained in a sad and defeated voice.

"Right. And Dr. Miner has long said his biggest regret was not having a son. I'm sure Rodney will be in good hands."

"Mason, the blame for poor Abigail was placed squarely on the shoulders of the mother, as if she had done something wrong. And why this obsession to have a son? What if Rodney disappoints? Would he still be shown love, caring? I think not. I'm very worried about this entire plan."

"Rachael, I've done my best for you. You might want to show a little appreciation for the trouble I've gone to, traveling back and forth between here and Abingdon......," Mason demanded as his voice drifted off.

13

"I'll agree only if I can stay in touch and the Miners under-stand this is temporary only. I'm not giving my son away!" Her voice was raised in both fear and indignation.

"Course not, course not. That's settled then." Mason was clearly happy to have this conversation end.

The children, except for Rodney and Susan, had listened to all this. Susan had taken Rodney outside to play so that he would not hear and get upset. None of them wanted to see sweet little Rodney go anywhere, especially not with Uncle Mason. Or even Uncle Ba-sil. Uncle Basil always agreed with everything Uncle Mason said. Somehow they just didn't trust either of them to be looking out for their best interest. And deep inside they knew their Papa would agree with that feeling.

Rachael was never aware her children knew of the plan to take Rodney away. When at last she had been faced with the dreaded moment of telling them, she had tried to make it all sound like a wonderful adventure and talked of the day when they would travel to Virginia by train to bring Rodney back to them. They pretended to be excited for their mother's sake.

The weeks rolled by and the only good news was that the war in Europe had ended. It was in November when they got this word and Rachael could for a few minutes rejoice for the families who would be welcoming home their husbands and sons. She knew how happy she would be if she thought Edward was coming home...... but that was not to be.

"Edward, Edward," she cried into her pillow, trying to muffle the sound of her sobs. She needed him so, and wondered if the ache and guilt of sending Rodney away would ever end. She had written to the Miners and received a terse reply and that only once. "Ronald is adjusting well" the note had said. Ronald, not Rodney. His name had been rejected, what about the little boy? Was he loved? Was he lonely? Was he afraid? Did he cry at night for his mother? The pain was more than Rachael could bear alone.

"Oh, Edward, I need you so." she cried again.

CHAPTER 3

Mrs. O'Donnell had requested a second year of leave to be with her baby, so Rachael continued in her teaching position. Toward the middle of her second year, she began to suspect the worse. Her symptoms were much like those of Edward when he first found he had tuberculosis. As much as she dreaded finding out the horrible truth, she knew she owed it to her children and her students to be certain. She had thought to be ready to make that long anticipated trip to Damascus to bring her darling Rodney home, but now knew the dream must be delayed one more time until she could be sure. Rachael traveled to Nashville to see a specialist.

"I'll be home in two days," she promised the children. They were very apprehensive of this separation, but trusted her words. She hoped to keep her problem a secret until the results would either deny or confirm. To her deepest sorrow, it was confirmed. Her homecoming brought only more tears to the "bravest little hearts in all Tennessee" according to their mother. Each child was affected differently and showed their grief and despair in separate ways. Steven walked out into the night and sat leaning against a big maple tree, starring at the sky, and wondering if somehow all this could be his fault? Had he been bad? Why was this happening to his family? What could he do to make things better?

"Steven," It was his mother calling to him. "Come in the house now, dear. It's bed time."

Steven ran to her and threw his arms around her waist. She stroked his back and kissed the top of his head.

"I know, my darling. I know. I'm so sorry, but we will always have our family, even though we may be apart. Family and love for one another are the most important things we have."

Mason and Basil White once more made their trip to Greeneville. They traveled in a new car, this one owned by Mason, which he described as the fanciest car in four states. It was very long with a big wheel on the back. It was a shiny gold color with black seats. There were lots and lots of silver trimmings on the sides. But as big as the car was, there was space for only two persons. Steven noted that Mason made a show of pointing that out to all the children. It was assumed they were being told they would not be offered a ride in his new automobile.

Rachael was deeply affected by her plight and offered almost no resistance to the plans laid out before her by her two brothers. She was in a subdued state and unable to make decisions on her own. The house was to be sold, as well as the store properties.

"I can't sell the house, or even the stores. It is my last connection to Edward. Isn't there someway we can keep them? Edward and I built this home to last us until we had grandchildren. The least I want to do is leave it for my own children." Rachael pleaded.

"That's just not possible. You have no way to support yourself or the children. They can't run the stores, which by the way have been closed for a while now and would not be a good investment." Basil told her.

Rachael had neither the stamina or the logic to argue the point. The stores had been closed for some time and she realized they had lost some of their value, but the house......her beautiful home she thought to live in for the rest of her life. She gave in to her brothers demands. The house and stores were sold. Rachael would be taken back to Washington County, VA in a location between Abingdon and Meadowview where Mason had found a good rental home. It was a small four room house but room enough for Rachael and Susan, who would stay with her mother as a nurse and helper.

"And we've good homes for all the boys," they assured her.

Rachael feared the 'good homes' were actually farmers in the area who needed a strong boy to do their dirty work. She had grown up in the Washington County area near Damascus and she had seen too many orphans taken in on the farms and worked very hard. Loving and caring folks treated a lucky few as family, but most often it was more of a servitude role. Just like the old indentured servants, who had little more rights than the slaves they worked along side, the orphans were 'hired' help and their only reward a meager room and board. Rachael didn't condone slavery any more than she could accept treating help unkindly. She had hoped for more for her chil-

16

CHAPTER 4

The family did take that train ride. The train ride they had been promised, a trip they thought to go and bring Rodney home. That long anticipated train ride to reunite had now turned into a ride with the two eldest brothers absent. Rachael held fast to Will as the train pulled away from the Greeneville station. Susan stayed close to her mother to help in any way she could. Steven, left to himself, pressed his face against the window and watched the familiar landscape roll out of sight. He didn't cry. He was confused, uncertain and afraid, but he didn't cry. He was thinking about a story his mother had told them, he thought it might have been from the Bible. The story was about a rich ruler who was killed along with his wife. Their bodies were cremated and 'their ashes were scattered on the wind' she had said.

"That's a little like what's happening to us," he thought. "we're scattered on the wind."

Each of the Williams passengers was leaving something behind. Rachael was leaving behind her home and the dream of a happy life with a man she loved. Susan was leaving behind her missed youth and unencumbered years. Will was leaving behind a world of confusion and loss which he didn't understand, but in his small world of hope believed he would be happy when the train stopped. Steven was leaving behind his life, his reason to exist, his family. No longer would they be one. His world had collapsed around him. He could only sit and watch the landscape as it went swiftly by, wanting this ride to go on forever.

The journey ended much too soon. It was not a long distance from their home in Tennessee to the town of Abingdon, Virginia, but Steven had hoped . He peered out the window at the depot. He didn't want to face what he knew lay ahead.

Steven could see his uncles, Mason and Basil, pacing about in front of the railroad station on the area he knew would be called 'the platform.' Their chins were tucked in their top coats as a chilling wind was blowing in the first signs of winter. From their expression it looked as though they wanted this to be over. Near them stood an elderly woman. Her clothing and dour expression reminded him of the Pilgrims whose faces were depicted in his school history book. She was small in stature and had Steven been more worldly he might have described her as having an aura of defeat about her. Two younger females accompanied her. The younger ones looked to be, perhaps, somewhere between their teens and very early twenties. Steven supposed the elder lady to be his mother's Aunt Nora. He already knew from discussions held before they left Tennessee that he would be going to live with her. He knew she was his mother's aunt, but still did not expect her to look so old. The two young women must be her daughters, Dottie and Frances. Steven had never met them, but couldn't help but notice how different their appearances were from one another. One wore a big smile and looked as thought she was having a good time. The other frowned and looked as if she had never had a happy day in her life nor did she expect one.

"Children, let's go," Rachael encouraged them. "Let's meet our family."

Steven didn't feel they were really family, but he knew he must go with them. At least for a little while until his mother was stronger.

"This one Steven?" Aunt Nora Carterson asked, nodding her head slightly in his direction. She neither frowned nor smiled. Her look could be better described as scrutiny.

"Yes," Rachael replied, pushing Steven forward. Will still clung to her other hand. "Steven is nine years old and a very good and caring son. You will love having him around. He is very smart and is an excellent helper." Rachael tried desperately to keep her voice lively and bright.

"How do you do, ma'am?" Steven asked, just as he had been instructed to do.

"Oh, isn't he polite?" beamed the smiling one. "Hello Steven, my name is Dottie. And this is my sister Frances."

"How do you do, ma'am?" Steven asked again. He knew you usually don't address a girl in her teens as ma'am, but he didn't know what else to say. He just wanted to climb back on the train and keep on riding, somewhere, anywhere away from here.

"Just call me Dottie, and I'll call you Steven." She was trying very hard to put the poor boy at ease. And as usual Frances wasn't helping. "Say hello, Frances. Steven is going to be living with us for awhile."

"You're smaller than I thought you were going to be," was all the ungracious Frances had to say. This raised a bit of a fight in Steven as he took it to be meant as an insult.

"Well, Bantam roosters are small too, but they got plenty of spunk," he said with spirit. Everyone laughed except Frances.

Steven's clothes had been packed separately so that he could leave immediately with the Cartersons while Uncles Mason and Basil were to take Rachael and Susan to the home they had rented. No one had shown up to claim Will.

"We should be going," Mason broke in. "We need to get Rachael settled in before dark. And this chill is not good for any of us." He moved his shoulders to illustrate, as though a chill had moved through his body.

"And we need to get started back ourselves. There's milking to be done and kindling wood to be brought in for morning." Aunt Nora said without emotion. Steven could imagine there were other chores she would have liked to add to the list, but maybe didn't think it was the time. Why did he get the feeling he was being considered only for the work he could do?

"Steven," his mother said with her emotions choked back, "be a good boy. Aunt Nora needs a man around the place for a while until her own son returns from overseas. He was a soldier in the war, you know. But the war has ended and he'll be coming home any day now. Try to help her all you can until his return, will you?" Nora's son, George, had been declared a prisoner of war and no records showed his whereabouts. It was unknown if he were dead or alive, but Nora insisted he'd be coming home and so everyone gave the appearance of believing the same fantasy.

Steven and his mother had talked many times before leaving Tennessee so he wasn't sure if she was uttering these words to reassure herself or him so he merely muttered, "Yes'm." He grabbed

21

his mother for one last embrace and bit his lip to stop the trembling.

He had never felt as empty as he felt now. Not even when Papa died. At least he had all the others around him. But now there was no one and he didn't think Frances was going to be a lot of help. He thought about poor little Rodney and how he too was alone. Steven wanted to cry, or yell, or pound his fist. Something, anything to make the emptiness in the pit of his stomach go away. He tried to straighten his back and still his quivering lips. Maybe Dottie would be his friend.

"Do you have any pets?" he asked, hoping to find some common ground with his new 'family.'

"We have a dog, his name is Pugg. And the cat is Miss Emily." Dottie smiled at the little boy and tried to make him feel welcome. But she knew in her heart he was going to find it very difficult to find a place in this family. They did not show emotion or love openly and withheld themselves as though it were a virtue.

After tearful goodbyes to his mother and sister, Steven climbed into the old automobile of the Cartersons and steeled himself to look straight ahead. His mother had promised to have someone come for him at the Carterson's farm and bring him to her for a visit. Maybe not this month, she had said, but surely next month when I am settled and rested. Steven held on to that thought.

But then he had another thought, remembering something that sent a true chill down his own spine. He had been so distraught, trying so hard to hold on without crying and holding on to his mother, he hadn't noticed where Will had gone. No one had shown up to claim Will.

CHAPTER 5

"No one has shown up to claim Will," Rachael said to her brothers. "I know you are anxious to be on our way, but this means I am taking Will with me."

"I'm sure there was a problem or they would be here. We'll get you set up at your house and then drop Will off with his new family on our way back home." Basil explained.

"I want to meet this family. I am not leaving my son with someone I don't know." Rachael insisted.

"We'll take you to visit the family this weekend, I promise. But it is really too far out of the way to go there, then back to your house and so forth. It just makes sense to take you and Susan home first." Mason added.

"No," insisted Rachael. But then she fell into a terrible coughing spell which left her very weak. Although she protested, she soon found herself being driven to the small house near Meadowview where she and Susan would live. Will was clinging to her in fear. Rachael's furniture wouldn't arrive for a few days but Mason or Basil had put together a few pieces to see them through. Rachael pulled up a sturdy looking kitchen chair and held Will on her lap.

"We'll talk with the folks and let them know you'll be coming by this weekend when you feel better. In the meantime, Will needs something to eat and to get settled in and have a good night's sleep. We'll all feel better about this in the morning." Basil and Mason were in agreement on these points. "Now let's get a fire built and get a little warmth in the house. Susan, my wife stocked some groceries in the pantry to get you started. Do you think you can fix your mother something once we get this fire going?"

"Of course I can," was her muted response. Susan was not surly, just very tired and very, very unhappy.

The two uncles drove away with little Will, leaving a sobbing and defeated Rachael. She made them vow they would come for her

23

on the weekend to see the home where Will would be living. It was a reluctant promise, but they made it.

On their journey back to Abingdon, the uncles took a detour toward a little town called Lodi. There they stopped at a decaying farm house with shutters hanging at varying angles. The yard was unkempt and trash abounded. There had once been a fence around the yard, but it had long ago fallen to ruin. A waft of dark smoke came from the chimney, assuring them someone was home and probably cooking supper on a wood burning cook stove.

"Howdy," Mason said when finally the door opened just a crack. His dialect was directed at the inhabitants, thinking them to be uneducated. "We got the youngin' you been expectin'," he said with a drawl.

"My husband says we can't take 'im in. That boy got the TB. You'ns didn't tell us he got the TB when you axed us to take 'im in. I got me two little girls. I can't let them git the TB" the woman told them.

"Oh no, this boy is healthy. I don't know where you got that idea," they protested.

This argument continued for several minutes; the uncles standing on the porch while the woman spoke to them through a mere crack in the door opening. At last the uncles persuaded her to allow the boy to remain, with the solemn promise they would be back on the weekend with his mother and the problem could be solved at that time. The woman agreed, reluctantly, and the uncles went away happy. They were determined to leave the boy there, and felt by the time they brought Rachael around to visit on the weekend they could come up with a 'plan of persuasion.' They had fulfilled their duty, they told themselves.

If they had looked over their shoulders as they drove away they would have seen a slovenly looking man, unshaven for many days and wearing a weather beaten hat, approaching the house. He entered the front door without knocking. Apparently he lived there.

"What's that youngin' a'doin here?" the bearded man shouted at his wife as he threw his hat on the table. "Didn't I tell ye we aint takin in no TB youngins?"

24

His wife tried to explain that Mr. Mason and Mr. Basil White would return on the weekend to pick the boy up. In the meantime, she would make sure he ate his meals separate from the rest. This was not what the man wanted to hear.

"No, you aint goin do no such thang. What good you thank a TB youngin' gonna do me? Sickly, can't work, 'sides probably make all us sickly too. Them White boys lied to me, said he'd be a good worker one day. Huh! You put that boy and his bags right out there on the porch. Onct I've et, I'll hitch up the horse and cart and I'm takin' him right back where he come from."

And that was the final say. His wife had experienced too many blows from his big hands, she knew when silence and obedience meant survival. Will was seated on the front porch with his small bundle of clothes at his feet.

The seat was cold and the wind blew harder. The chill had reached within his very soul, but still Will sat motionless. He had no where to go, and even at his young age he knew begging to come inside was not an option open to him. So he just sat, swinging his legs in the cold, and trying to think of other things. Think about ole Fritz. He had hated leaving his dog behind. He had hoped there would be a nice dog at his new home. But now where was that new home? He guessed this one wasn't where he was supposed to be.

He noted a car going down the road, a pretty old car, a lot like his Papa's. He paid little attention, he knew no one in these parts, but did think it funny to see an old woman driving. He thought only men knew how to drive a car. He had never seen a woman driving in Greeneville. He continued to stare out into the distance, noticing it was growing darker and hoped the man would get the horse hitched up and come and get him before too much longer.

The same car returned. The old woman got out and appeared to rush toward him. He was afraid. Who was she? She was very large and untidy but her face looked nice. Friendly. And right now, Will needed a friend.

"Hold ever-*thang*, hold ever-*thang*. Would you be Edward and Rachael Williams kin?" she asked breathlessly.

"My momma's name is Rachael. We come from Greeneville,

Tennessee." Will answered respectfully.

"Well, I'm some kin to your daddy, rest his soul. I heard you youngins was a comin today and the White boys been huntin homes for ye in these parts. I just wondered when I saw ye sittin' here with your bag you just might be my kin. Folks around here just call me Miss Alvira."

"I'm ha—happy to know you." Will chattered. He was growing very cold.

"Can you set here just one minute while I speak to them folks inside?" she asked him, lowering her voice as though she did not wish to be overheard. He agreed. Where else could he go?

Will heard a lot of shouting from inside. Most of it was Miss Alvira's voice and she didn't sound too happy with current events. The shouting stopped suddenly and Miss Alvira returned to the front porch. As she did so, she dropped to one knee before little Will. She touched his cheeks, cold and red, and smoothed away the strands of hair that had escaped his cap.

"Oh, laddie, I have been so wantin' to meet ya. I got this big old house and it's so empty." She said this with the tenderness of one who has much love to give and her eyes told the same story.

"Th - Then are yo - you the one who's going to take care of me?" Will asked hopefully, trying to control the chattering of his teeth. His words were barely audible.

"Only if you let me, laddie. I got much carin' to give and you look like you just the young fellow I want to share it with."

Will was holding on to Alvira's hand in sheer desperation. This blustery woman had scared him half to death, and he was already near faint when she appeared. But now he saw only her merciful act as she tucked him snuggly in the front seat of her old car and pulled a ragged blanket around him.

"Wait til I get you home, laddie. We'll build up the fire and put the kettle on. Bet a cup of hot tea will fix you up! Or maybe you're a bit too young for tea. Bet I can find a bit of soup. That sounds better, now don't it, laddie?" Alvira kept talking in an attempt to keep the boy awake. His eyelids had already began to droop, and she wanted to get some hot food in his little stomach before putting him to bed for the night.

"Do you have a dog?" Will asked. " I had a dog named Fritz, but I couldn't bring him with me."

"Yeah, I got a dog. Can't have a farm without a dog. Name's Willie. Then I got two, maybe three cats, but they got no names. Maybe you'd like to name 'em for me? And then I got these goats that like to come in the yard and eat my flowers. They got little kids so I reckon you could call 'em pets, too. And the calves. And then there's the colt due any day now…….." Alvira's voice drifted off as she could see her little passenger was already fast asleep.

When the White brothers arrived at the ram shackled house on the weekend, Rachael's heart sank as her eyes took in the decay of the place. How could her brothers have been so heartless as to place a small child in this environment? Her dismay turned to sheer panic when she learned Will was not there. The group retraced their steps to the car, and left at full speed to find Alvira's place.

"Miss Alvira?" Rachael asked in disbelief. She had not seen the woman in many years and was shocked at her appearance. Alvira's hair was mostly gray and wispy and could be described only as total disarray. She had put on a lot of weight over the years and her blouse buttons barely met and strained to be free. She wore galoshes on her feet, as thought she had just come in from the barn.

"Momma, Momma!" It was a happy, smiling, well-scrubbed little boy who rushed to hug his mother. "Wait till I tell you about all the animals. We've got everything. It's just like Old MacDonald's Farm that you taught us. Is this where I'm going to stay for awhile, Momma? With Miss Alvira?"

"Yes, darling, if that's what Miss Alvira wants. I know she is going to take very good care of you. I just know it." Rachael felt happy for the first time in weeks. At least one of her children had found love.

Steven didn't know of the cruel events surrounding his younger brother, nor did he know of the happy ending. He had thought about Will a lot during the last weeks and wondered where he might be. It wasn't until the third Sunday of the month rolled around that he would learn of Will's fate. The Circuit Preacher was

27

due each third Sunday and that's the Sunday Aunt Nora's family attends the Green Springs Baptist Church. As it happens, Miss Alvira has the same routine and arrived minutes after the Carterson party, bringing her new ward, little Will.

Steven couldn't believe his eyes. Will saw Steven at just about the same moment. The two brothers rushed to each other and embraced. People stopped to look but neither boy cared. Steven knew he was too old to cry in public, so he blinked real hard, over and over. His little brother was safe and sound. And he was near.

CHAPTER 6

Steven was trying very hard to fit into life on the Carterson farm. On that first day's ride from the rail station in Abingdon they had traveled over winding roads until they came to a fenced-in pasture with a mailbox by the gate.

"This is where the farm begins," Dottie had explained to him. "The house sits back a ways. During the school year, Mother will ask you to pick up the mail for her on your way home."

Dottie had tried to keep Steven's spirits up as they made that first journey to his new home. He had learned then that Dottie attended the Stonewall Jackson Institute, a boarding school in Abingdon, and was only home for a few days to welcome him. Frances had tried boarding school for a few weeks but found it 'disagreeable' and had returned home. He wished it had been Frances who lived elsewhere. But at least Dottie would be home during the holidays and summers.

Steven could recall his first impression of the farmhouse. As they bumped along over rutted ground, then suddenly topped a small rise, Steven had his first glimpse of the house nestled in the hollow. One end of the house appeared to be of the original log, with an addition of clapboard. A long porch connected the two structures. Two huge chimneys reached toward the sky. There were many assorted outbuildings, some of which Steven could identify, others he wasn't sure.

The weeks seemed to crawl slowly and sadly along.

"Get up boy. Breakfast is ready." Aunt Nora rose early and started the fire in the kitchen cook stove each morning. Steven was responsible to see that she always had plenty of kindling and starter wood before he went to bed each night.

"We got pancakes this morning," she added.

Steven quickly climbed from under his covers and drew on his trousers. His sleeping quarters was a loft over the kitchen, so warmth in the winter wasn't a problem. At least in the early evening hours. Before morning the coldness would creep in and in the deepest of winter he expected the snow would most likely blow right in to cover his blankets with a fine powder. But Steven was growing immune to the coldness, both physically and emotionally. He didn't receive nor did he expect love. He was beginning to forget what it meant to be loved. Maybe it was just a fantasy that some children have.

He scrambled down the ladder and took his place at the table. Aunt Nora piled four buckwheat cakes on his plate and he covered them with the hot liquid she made from boiling brown sugar with water. They filled his stomach and satisfied his longing for the sweet taste from another time in his young life.

"Can I have more?" he asked when he had finished his plate.

"How many more you want? You need to get on with your chores. You can't sit and eat all day." Aunt Nora was not one to spoil, that was certain. But a growing boy can eat more than one small plate of pancakes. She put more cakes on Steven's plate, showing in her actions that she was doing this but didn't approve. He ate in silence. The joy of the moment had slipped away.

Steven left the table and went about his daily routine. He fed the dog, Pugg. Pugg was a big disappointment. He was a bulldog who looked about a thousand years old and spent his days curled up behind the kitchen cook stove. Aunt Nora said he was 'along in years' and didn't like to be played with much. Steven wasn't much interested in playing with Pugg either. And as for Miss Emily the cat, she belonged to Frances and spent all her time napping on Frances' bed. Steven didn't have to take care of that one.

Steven did his share of the milking, put down some hay, slopped the hogs, fed the chickens, and any other duties expected of him as assigned by Aunt Nora. Later, he would haul water from the spring and fill all the tubs needed and chop kindling wood for the next day.

Steven was enrolled in school, but found it was a very long walk. Back in Tennessee, he had walked only during his first year, but by grade two his mother was teaching and they went together in the automobile. But now, he found his new school was several miles from the Carterson farm, and the winter months was making the trip a painful one. Some days his feet would ache from the coldness. But once in class he felt the long journey worth it. Will was enrolled in the same school and that meant seeing his brother every day, or at least every week day. Steven was a good student and his teachers were proud of him. It was the only time he was truly happy.

"Want one of my ham biscuits?" Will would ask most days.

"I surely do. You know all I get is apple butter biscuits, but I've got one of those for you, too." Steven would tell him.

Miss Alvira certainly provided Will with a more tantalizing noon day meal, even if her biscuits couldn't hold a candle to Aunt Nora's. But between the two boy's pails, they both ended with a nourishing meal and the best part was the sweet treats that Miss Alvira would sometimes slip into Will's pail. After Will had told her of Steven's scant offering, she always added an extra treat for Steven, too. Steven's favorite was the hard rock candy while Will preferred the taffy.

A stranger approached the Carterson house late one afternoon. He was wearing some sort of uniform often worn by the telegram people in Abingdon. The stranger knocked on the door of the farmhouse. The family had witnessed his arrival, but no one wanted to go to the door. It might be bad news. The war department would send a telegram when it was bad news. What if they had finally discovered the whereabouts of George? And what if they found, while he was held prisoner, he had died? Aunt Nora and Frances stared at each other, neither could move. Steven went to the door.

"This here the Carterson place?" asked the irritated delivery man.

"Yes."

"Got a telegram here. I need somebody to sign," was his curt reply. Steven would have expected more kindness from someone bringing bad news, but kept quiet. Aunt Nora rose and came to sign where the rude young man indicated.

Closing the door, she slowly opened the telegram. But instead of weeping, a slow smile spread over her face. Steven was shocked. He had never seen her smile before. This telegram must

31

truly be good news.

"My boy. George. George is being released from the hospital, it says. Oh, he's safe, he's safe..... and he's coming home."

Frances, her own face showing an infrequent smile, hugged her mother. They were overjoyed by this good news. They read the telegram over and over. They tried to calculate his day of arrival. And they asked themselves many times why he was in the hospital? The prisoners of war had been released months before, and returned to the states. Why was George not among them? It would be weeks before they would know the whole story.

"We'll be sure Dottie is home for this occasion," they both agreed.

The farm was thrown into a tizzy. Even though it was not quite spring, the spring cleaning began anyway and in earnest. All would be made ready for the returning son and the poor brother who had no doubt suffered untold atrocities at the hands of the unholy heathen, those being Frances' words.

"What's George like?" asked Steven. He avoided asking the obvious which would be 'is he more like Dottie or more like you?' If Steven could have described Frances the words he might have used would be sour, uppity and definitely destined to be an old maid.

"What do you mean?" Frances was busy polishing the floor and didn't have time for stupid questions.

"I just meant, what does he like to do? Does he whittle? Or play music? Does he have any hobbies?" asked Steven.

"Well, he always like to hunt. Especially rabbits or squirrels. And he likes to walk in the woods in the fall of the year. You know, when all the leaves are so colorful. Guess he just likes things natural. 'Bout all I can tell you." Frances was not in the habit of talking to Steven, seeming to feel he was more a servant than a family member and polite conversation was not a requirement. This was probably the longest continuous speech she had shared with him.

"I'm sure excited about him coming home. Seems like it'll make Aunt Nora happy." Steven said. He was answered with only a grunt from Frances, clearly she did not think Steven's opinion of the occasion to be a matter of importance.

32

Steven took his cue from her and left the room. As far as Frances was concerned he wasn't a party to this glorious occasion of her brother's return. Steven had for a few days been caught up in the excitement, but now steeled himself to be the outsider once again. Sort of like he had felt at Christmas.

At last the day dawned when George was to arrive home by train. The family had learned through correspondence with the army doctors as to the problems with getting George home sooner. When the prisoners had been released, George was only partially conscious. He had suffered a severe head wound as well as malnutrition. His resistance was low and his body was an easy target for pneumonia. George suffered what they deemed to be a temporary memory loss due to the combination head wound and high fever. It was several months before the mass of paperwork came through to give them positive identification of the soldier in their care. And only now was he finally able to travel to return to his family. His wounds were healed, and while he still showed signs of his torturous times, they could do no more. He needed the love and support of his family. He was coming home.

The family waited impatiently in the Abingdon depot, peering out it's many windows. They had dressed in their finest, wanting George to feel this was a momentous occasion. They were as excited as they were ever apt to be, considering their reluctance at showing emotion. Steven remembered his own arrival at this train station, but pushed those unhappy thoughts from his mind. He believed things could only get better by having a man around the house.

"Lookie, here it comes," squealed Frances. She referred to the smoke which could be seen in the distance, acknowledging the train's imminent arrival. As one, the body of persons awaiting the train rushed outside.

"Stand back. Don't need to get nobody killed," cautioned Aunt Nora. But while her words were stern, her face gave away her own excitement. She was truly thrilled to have her son returning.

It seemed to take an eternity for the train to pull into the station and when finally the conductors disembarked and put down the little steps that would help the passengers to leave the train, all the Cartersons felt the strain of the long wait.

"Do you see him?" asked Dottie.

"No, I'm looking but I don't see him," answered Frances, frantically.

They ran about, looking into all the cars. Most of the passengers who were due to exit the train had long since disembarked. Could it be something had caused George's trip to be delayed? Their faces sagged with disappointment.

"Look, there he is!" cried Aunt Nora. She pointed to a man slowly leaving the train, leaning on the conductor for assistance.

"Momma, I don't see him. Oh no, you don't mean........." Dottie's voice trailed off. She was looking at a skeleton of a man, not the robust brother she remembered.

What in the world has happened to him, Momma?" asked Frances.

"Never mind. Don't you act as if anything is wrong. He has been through a lot. He's going to be alright," their mother told them.

And so the family gathered around George and gave him warm hugs and kisses on the cheek. Their smiles held, but were not returned. George looked at them as total strangers. The only one not surprised was Steven. Since he had never met George, he didn't know what else to expect so just accepted him as he was. And George accepted Steven in the same manner. Two strangers, one meaning nothing to the other. They were polite.

The ride home was uneventful and George spoke only in monosyllables. Dottie chatted away to cover the uncomfortable silence and tried to bring George up to date on the happenings around the farm since he had gone away.

"I guess Momma wrote and told you the old mule, Ferdie, had died. But we got a brand new plow horse. I think you'll like him. And Elsie just had a new calf. It's the prettiest one yet."

She didn't know if George was actually listening, but felt it better to keep talking and ignore his strange behavior. She knew her brother had suffered a great deal during this war and was thankful it had ended. But she did think he would feel some emotion at being safely home again.

Aunt Nora had cooked for days to make the homecoming special, but no one showed much of an appetite. Steven could eat all he wanted for once without his Aunt Nora chiding him about wasting food.

It had been a tiring and emotionally draining day for all, and so they retired to bed a bit earlier than usual. They were all sleeping when suddenly they awoke to blood curdling screams. Steven scrambled down from his loft and ran to the front porch in only his long Johns. There stood George, holding on tight to the porch rail and screaming as loudly as anyone could. The others had rushed out too, in their nightclothes and bare feet and stood staring. For a minute no one spoke, then Aunt Nora stepped forward and placed her hands gently on his shoulders.

"Come, son. Come with me. You're home now." She led him back to his own bed.

Nothing was ever said about the incident, but it was to be repeated night after night for many weeks. Steven no longer rushed down from the loft when he heard the screams.

CHAPTER 7

Weeks flew by and soon George did begin to talk and take a more active interest in the farm. It was good to have another set of hands to help out with some of the chores, but Steven found George could not always be depended on. George really tried, but sometimes he would simply forget, other times he would go into a mood Aunt Nora called 'depression.' On those days, George couldn't be counted on at all.

"Want to go for a walk?" Steven asked him one day. He didn't know if George would reply but he wanted to try to know him better and remembered what Frances had said about him liking to hunt and take walks in the woods.

"Yeah, sounds good." George replied, surprisingly.

They walked for several minutes in silence. Then George saw something that rekindled an old memory. He began showing Steven his favorite walnut tree, the one that always grew the walnuts with the biggest kernels. And a small stream where the beavers loved to build their dams. It was a great afternoon, one Steven would remember for all his life, when the true George of the past came back for a short while.

"Let's do this again sometime," George told him when they returned to the house to begin their evening chores. Steven hoped he had found a friend.

Months rolled along and soon it would be Christmas. There had not been much of a celebration last year because Aunt Nora had declared it a year of mourning until George returned. There had been no decorations, and only one or two gifts exchanged among Aunt Nora, Dottie and Frances. Steven had been sad about that, remembering all the gaiety from his own family memories, but he tried to be brave. This year was to be special. The house was full of greenery and good smells from the kitchen.

Steven found Christmas Day with the Carterson's to be the worst day of his new life. He had grieved for Papa, he had grieved when he had to leave his mother, but on this Christmas he knew just how much he had lost.

Aunt Nora and Frances had returned from Abingdon, with their shopping bags spilling over with interesting looking parcels. With George's help, they put up a big cedar tree in the parlor, and gifts were placed under the tree. They were wrapped in white tissue with some of them sporting red or green ribbons. Steven watched with glee, not daring to investigate the gifts. He had been warned not to touch!

He had whittled a new rolling pin for Aunt Nora. It was made from a single piece of wood, sanded and polished just so. Steven was anxious for his Aunt Nora to open it. He hoped she'd be pleased. The smells of Christmas were making him happy, the smell of the cedar and pine, of cakes in the oven, Steven was getting excited as he remembered so many wonderful holidays at home, when all of his own family were still together.

After breakfast on Christmas morning, all gathered to open gifts. Dottie was home for the holidays and began to hand out the presents. Many big packages were presented, to Frances, to George, to Aunt Nora and some she placed in a stack for herself. The ladies opened boxes of new "pumps" which is what the girls called their new shoes with heels. There were fancy pocketknives for George, and neckties. There were pretty nightgowns, dresses and the hats that Frances called the latest style for the 'flapper,' whatever that might be. There were many *oohs* and *aahs*, as the gifts were opened but none of them had come Steven's way. Aunt Nora had not expressed the joy Steven had hoped for when she opened his gift, but she *almost* smiled when she said 'thank you.' Or maybe he imagined it. He would have to be satisfied with that.

At last there was only one large package under the tree. Since he had none, he just knew it would be his. But then Dottie handed it to Aunt Nora. When Dottie removed the larger package, Steven could see two very small gifts which had been hidden. His heart had dropped to his toes as he saw all the gifts being given to someone else, but at least there was still a chance. He had hoped for one of the big presents like everyone else had gotten. He had heard the boys at school talking about some of the things they had asked to find under the tree on Christmas.   Rifles, fishing poles, so many things a boy might want.

His mind went back to his years in Greeneville, when he had lived a happy life with his parents.   He could recall Harold getting his first rifle, of Randolph getting his first bicycle.   He didn't know what Aunt Nora had in mind for him; he didn't expect it to be one of the more expensive choices.   But even a small package could hold a good pocket knife, maybe even a larger jack knife.   And sure enough, Dottie was coming his way with one of the small packages.   His heart was beating fast.   He was still smarting some over not being included all morning with the family gift exchange, but at least now there was hope he had not been totally overlooked.   He slowly opened his gift, wanting to make the moment last.   It was going to be his only moment, and he wanted to hold it.   He tore the paper back and gazed at his gift……..it was a comb.

Aunt Nora and Frances put their gifts aside and went to the kitchen to start the Christmas dinner.   George collected his gifts and retired to his own room, which was his habit and now accepted by all.   Only Dottie remained and only Dottie saw the tears.   Steven didn't understand why this was happening.   He shared their home, did all he could to help.   He felt as if he were invisible, until there was work to be done.   Why? What had he done?   He vowed he would never treat another person this way.

"You have one more gift, Steven.   This one is from me." Dottie told him. As she spoke she handed him the last little gift from under the tree. It was a pair of socks she had knitted for him.   " I know how cold your feet can get when you're walking to school."

He hugged her hard and said, "Thank you, Dottie," and turned his face away.   He did not want his only friend in the family to see him cry.

CHAPTER 8

One day as Steven was in the barn cleaning the stalls; Aunt Nora paid him an unexpected visit. She didn't much like coming to the barn, leaving the milking and haying up to him or to George on his good days. Today she had a strange look on her face.

"Steven, I've asked George to drive us to see your mother. I've received word that she is not doing well. We will make the trip and see her at once."

Steven thought he might have heard a hint of a tear in her voice, but couldn't be sure. But one thing was sure, Aunt Nora was dropping everything to go at once. This had to mean his mother was very sick indeed. Tossing his pitch fork aside, he ran to the house to wash the dirt and manure away. He put on his only good trousers and his shoes and ran to the automobile. Aunt Nora and George were waiting.

The trip seemed to take forever. George drove slowly and carefully. More than once Steven had the urge to get out and run to his mother. At long last George turned off the road and parked in front of a small house. Susan was watching from the open doorway.

As soon as the automobile had stopped, Steven leaped from it and burst toward the front door of the little house. At first he glanced only momentarily at his sister. But now he looked once again. She had aged , she didn't look like a young girl anymore. There were dark circles under her eyes and her body appeared frail. Her hair hung limply about her shoulders. Steven wanted to reach out to her.

"Go, Steven, she's waiting," was Susan's only comment to the anxious boy.

"Momma!" he cried as he ran to her. Rachael was propped up on pillows, most likely placed there by Susan, and he could see the tears streaming down her face.

"I saw you coming from a distance," she said. "I knew it was your Aunt Nora's vehicle and I prayed I was going to see my big boy." She wiped the hair back from Steven's forehead and kissed him there.

"Momma, are you real sick?" Steven asked. There was hope in his voice that he would hear good news.

"Yes, darling, I am. I will be so sorry to leave you but the doctor doesn't think that I will get well."

And indeed Rachael Williams was not going to get well. The strain of the absence and heartbreak of worrying about her children had taken its toll on her health. The necessary rest she needed would be denied her as she spent the nights sleepless and crying over their welfare.

" Try to get her to rest," the doctor had told Susan.

"I am trying, but she is so worried. What am I to do?" Susan would reply, helplessly. "She walks the floor and cries, day after day, night after night. What am I to do?" When Susan broke down in heartbreaking sobs, he had quit insisting.

The doctor had tried talking to Rachael, taking the pressure off Susan. He knew the child was doing her best. On this day, Rachael was seated in front of her window, rocking gently back and forth, staring out but clearly not focusing. Her thoughts were miles away.

"Rachael," the doctor began softly, "I would like for you to try this medication. You must rest. Your body demands it if you are to gain any strength at all."

"You didn't know my husband, Edward, did you?" she asked him, apparently not hearing his comments. Her mind was elsewhere. "He was a wonderful man."

"No, I didn't know him," the doctor replied. He felt it best to let her talk it out and he was a good listener.

"Edward wanted Harold to go on to school, maybe even be a doctor. Harold is very bright. All of my children are good students. We had such dreams of what they would become," she told him.

"I'm sorry, Rachael," was all the doctor had said. He knew she had more to say.

"Rodney was such a beautiful baby. Everyone loved him. I

42

wish I could hold him again. I need him to be with me. And poor Susan. I have made a drudge of her. She should have lovely dresses, and even have a beau. Instead she is carrying water and firewood to take care of a sick mother. It isn't fair," she told him.

"No, Rachael, it isn't fair." There were no words of comfort he could give her. The despair was too deep, all he could do was listen.

"I wonder where Randolph is now? He's so good with numbers, you know. Edward wanted him to follow in his footsteps, mathematics at Carson-Newman," she said to no one in particular. "And little Steven and Will....................." her voice drifted off. She continued to rock, staring but seeing nothing at all, unaware of another presence in the room. Finally, when the doctor knew he could not be of help, he had left.............................

Rachael was not going to get well.

"Tell me about your new home, Steven. I'm sure Aunt Nora is taking very good care of you." Rachael said this with so much sorrow mixed with hope in her voice, Steven didn't have the heart to tell her the truth. Besides, Aunt Nora had entered the room now and it wouldn't pay to make her mad.

And so Steven told his mother about the fighting red rooster and the many apple trees and all the things he knew she needed to hear. He didn't speak of the many nights he had been so tired and hungry, cold and alone, and had cried unashamedly before mercifully falling asleep. Rachael stroked her son's head and tried to smile away her tears as she listened to his brave little lies, her heart breaking.

"Why don't you read to me, Steven? I'd really like that," she asked.

And so Steven read until Rachael fell into a deep and needed sleep.

"Is she dead?" cried Steven in fear.

"No," his sister Susan replied, "she is just sleeping, Steven. You did a good thing for Momma. This is the nicest sleep she has had in a very long time."

43

Steven held his mother's hand and watched her sleep until Aunt Nora said it was time to go. They would try to come back again as soon as possible, most likely the next Sunday. Steven left with this silent promise to his mother. He was glad he had helped her.

But next Sunday's visit was not to be. George was having one of his worst attacks. George was not in condition to go, and the remainder of the family dared not leave him behind. Before Steven was to have his second visit with his mother, word came that she had passed away quietly in her sleep. The next time Steven would be with her would be once again, at a train depot, this time when they traveled in a separate rail car, back to Greeneville for her burial beside her husband in the yard of stones at the Mount Zion Baptist Church.

CHAPTER 9

The years passed rather uneventfully and Steven was now reaching his full height at the age of fifteen. He graduated school, that being only through the eighth grade. His teacher had wept, wanting him to go on to higher learning, but Steven knew that was impossible. He did regret he would no longer see his classmates, and most of all he would miss seeing his brother Will on a regular basis. But now that the boys were older, Miss Alvira promised to let Will ride the horse over for a visit some Sundays. And Aunt Nora, being put on the spot, agreed that maybe Steven could borrow the wagon 'once in a while' and ride over to Will's house, that too, being on a Sunday when his work load was lessened.

Steven knew his sister Susan had entered the Johnston Memorial School of Nursing in Abingdon. The Pastor of the church in Meadowview who served on the Board of Directors there for several years, had persuaded the Administrator to give Susan a full scholarship. Susan's faithful time of caring for her mother had not gone unnoticed and now a very influential man was rewarding her. Steven saw Susan on a couple of occasions and she seemed to be very happy with the arrangement and her role as nurse. She expressed a desire to nurse in a tuberculosis hospital when her training was complete. She was writing to a new and very modern hospital in Philadelphia. If she got the position it would take her many miles away, but she promised to stay in touch.

Dottie graduated school too, her diploma being from the finishing school in Abingdon. But rather than returning home, Dottie announced she was engaged and a wedding had taken place a few weeks later. Steven was happy for her even though he would miss her cheery presence in an otherwise severe atmosphere. She and her new husband moved to Richmond, Virginia where he was to join a law firm.

George's 'spells' as Aunt Nora chose to call them, had grown less frequent but had grown more violent. George often broke or smashed things. Aunt Nora tried to keep him occupied and happy

45

while Steven just tried to stay out of his way. And such a pity too. The two, George and Steven, had many good times together, mostly just walking about the farm observing the beauty of nature. George loved the land and nature unspoiled. Steven thought it might be because of his years as a prisoner. George had long since ceased to be any help around the farm. No one asked it of him. Aunt Nora brought in hired help as needed with the heavy farming. Otherwise, Steven kept things going on a day-to-day basis.

On a warm summer day while Steven was out hoeing corn, he spotted a man walking down the rutted roadway leading to the house. His clothes appeared to be rather shabby and Steven knew he had never seen this man before. As the stranger drew closer, Steven realized the man was a Negro.

"Ma'am" the man spoke humbly when he reached Aunt Nora where she stood watching from her porch. "I wuz a wonderin' ifen yu had some work. I be's aworkin' for food, ma'am." The man bowed his head as he spoke and his eyes were affixed to something on the ground just beyond where Aunt Nora was standing. The man held a battered hat in his hands which he nervously turned around and around.

"Well, there's always wood to chop." Aunt Nora said, as if to dismiss the man totally. She motioned for Steven to join them. "Steven, show him where the wood pile is and get the axe and whatever else he needs." With those words she went back inside the house.

Steven told the man to follow him and in minutes the wood was being split. Steven was amazed at how fast the man could work with seemingly small effort.

"What's your name?" Steven asked.

"Joe," the man said, looking straight at Steven and smiling, "What's your name?"

"Steven"

"That your Ma?" he asked, friendly like.

"No, my ma, mother is dead. That's my Aunt Nora."

"Sorry," the man rested on the axe handle momentarily as he said this and looked at Steven. "My mother is dead too.. It is a very sad thing."

"How come you talk different to me than you was talkin' to Aunt Nora?" Steven asked.

"A man who got a family to feed must do whatever it take," he said simply.

"But you talked like you didn't have any schoolin'. But now you talk plain."

"I had schoolin', son. My mother was raised in the north and had as good an education as most. She taught me." Joe explained.

"Then why……..."

"Steven, look at me. What do you see?" Joe stopped chopping and stood looking at the Steven.

"I see a man who's supposed to be chopping wood but he's leaning on his axe." Steven answered mischievously.

"Ah, that's my point. You said 'I see a man.' Now most white folks look and say 'I see a worthless lazy no-account nigga.' That's what most folks say."

"Then why did you act like you was stupid? You held your head down, you didn't look Aunt Nora in the eye like you do me."

"'Cause, Steven, I needed the work. I need to feed my family. White folks don't take too kindly to a colored man lookin' them in the eye. They take it to mean we bein' 'uppity' and it scares them. So we stare at the ground, and make sure we don't make eye contact."

"That's the dumbest thing I ever heard," Steven protested.

"Maybe, but it true. If I really want some work and food for the table, I gots to play along. Or I be told to be on my way. And I need this work," Joe said.

"You didn't ask Aunt Nora what she was going to pay you. Why not?"

"Cause I will have to accept whatever she feel she want to give me. To make demands for your work ain't gonna help matters. She would have turned me away with nothin'." Joe explained. Steven obviously had never dealt with anyone other than the few white hands Aunt Nora hired and this experience was a bit overwhelming to him. But he was deeply interested in everything Joe had to say.

Just as they were speaking of Joe's reward for work, Aunt

47

Nora was apparently having the same thoughts as she came out into the yard and called Steven to come to the house for a few minutes.

"I want you to get a sack out of the barn and put some of that side meat from the smokehouse in it. Some of the outside pieces are getting rancid. Cut those off and give them to the nig…..the man." Aunt Nora instructed him.

"What else?" asked Steven. He hoped surely that was not all she planned to give the man who had worked so hard and fast.

"We got extra eggs we can't use?" Aunt Nora asked.

"Yeah, a lot of them, Aunt Nora. I'll pick out the oldest ones." Steven was catching on to how this was going to be. "And we got some turnips that is shriveled and no account. How about I add some of them? And some apples we put up last fall is beginning to turn too. I could throw those in."

"Well, let's not overdo it." Aunt Nora warned.

"Nah, guess you're right. Them apples is only fit for the hogs. I'll go ahead and put them in with the slop after supper." Steven was lying, but enjoying every minute of it.

"Well, I guess if you have to throw them out anyway. The apples might have turned, but if you're careful you can get enough good pieces for at least one pie. Go ahead and put them in Joe's sack, but be sure they're the turned ones," she said. She actually was glad Steven had brought these two items to her attention. She could go to her Baptist Women's Missionary Meeting and tell them how she had given this shiftless person a big bag of food for his hungry children.

When Joe was near to finishing his work, Steven ran back to the barn for the sack. Taking the bag to the root cellar, he quickly dug out several of their finest apples saved all winter in the warm straw. Then he placed several very large turnips on top of these, but he took along some of the wilted turnip tops in case he needed them for cover. Going to the smokehouse, he sliced off as many good slices of ham that he dared. Next he placed the wilted turnip greens on top of the good ham, covering it well, then placed the rancid ham on top of this. He put a dozen fresh laid eggs in a separate box. He proudly presented his bounty to Joe.

48

"What you been up to, Steven?" Joe asked suspiciously.

"You worked for food, you got food. It might not be just exactly the way Aunt Nora explained it to me, but then let's just say I'm only fifteen and I don't always listen too good."

Joe laughed and swung the bag over his shoulder. He carried the eggs in his other hand. When he reached the front of the house, he paused to wait for Aunt Nora to put in her appearance. Joe quickly took off his hat and began to twist it in his hands, shuffling his feet , with bowed head and eyes toward the ground, he thanked her for her charity.

"My chillin' gwinna eat good tonite, missy. And I shorely thank ye," he said.

Aunt Nora noted the bag looked a little full and said she wished to view what Steven had 'paid' Joe for his services. Looking into the bag she saw only the rancid meat and the wilted turnip tops. Just as she and Steven had discussed. She bade Joe farewell and told him to stop in again when there was work to be done.

Joe once again slung the bag over his shoulder and walked slowly down the rutted road leading him from whence he came. Steven followed along beside him for a ways.

"Joe, you know that spot down the road, by the Wheeler's spring house? They's a big rock long side the road. Will you wait there for me for a bit?" Steven asked.

"What you up to? You sound like you got somethin' goin' on." Joe asked suspiciously.

"Just wait." And with that Steven went back toward the house. He pretended to be going to fetch water, but instead cut into the root cellar and filled a second sack with some of their best potatoes. "Should have thought of this sooner," was his only comment to himself. Satisfied he had enough he took out across the orchard, well out of sight of the main house. He used this trail as a short cut to school, and knew it well. As he rounded the corner of the barn, he spied some chickens scratching in the dirt. On impulse he grabbed one up quickly and before it could do a lot of squawking, he had wrung it's neck.

"If I'm caught, I'm goin' get a lickin' so I might as well make

49

the lickin' worth while." He was having more fun fooling his Aunt Nora than he had had in a long time.

When he caught up to Joe at the spring house, Joe was reluctant to take the second sack and was especially leery of accepting the chicken Steven had dangling from his other hand.

"Take it, Joe.   You really did earn it.   And as far as Aunt Nora goes, she already checked your bag and she okayed what was in it.   And she saw you go across the hill from the house.   She knows you weren't carryin' no chicken."

"And what if you get in trouble?" Joe asked.

"Been in trouble before.   'Sides, I don't think Aunt Nora would ever miss a few potatoes and we got lots of foxes here abouts that get into our chickens."

The temptation for a few good meals for his family was too much for Joe and he accepted the gifts gratefully.

"If you ever need a friend, you've got one in me, Steven Williams. I'll never forget you," was all he said as he tucked the chicken into the bag with the potatoes. Wouldn't do to let folks see him walking down the road with such a prize.   They'd call the sheriff for sure.

Steven went back home the same way he had come and filled the water bucket at the spring.   He carried it to the house and began filling the tubs.   He couldn't help but whistle while he worked.

CHAPTER 10

Steven wrote to his brother Randolph several times after their mother's death. He had been surprised that Randolph had left his logging job and was now working in North Carolina at a furniture factory. Aunt Martha had continued to write to Randolph and notified him of his mother's death. He had been the first to arrive.

Their mother's funeral was the only time Steven had seen Randolph since he'd moved to Aunt Nora's. Miss Alvira had volunteered to accompany her little Will to the funeral, and Steven and Susan had stayed close by their side. The reunion was bittersweet. The four children stayed at Aunt Martha's house where they talked long into the night. Aunt Martha, knowing they needed their time together, put pallets on the floor where they could be together. Most of the talk was regrets for the loss of their parents and their past life with them, with some mention of the loneliness they had experienced of late. And then they had all gone their separate ways once again.

Since that time Randolph had kept in touch and Steven still had a visit from Will fairly often. Susan, after completing the requirements at the nurses school in Abingdon, had been accepted at the Philadelphia hospital she had talked about. Steven was going to have to find his old geography books to trace his own family. First High Point, North Carolina and now Philadelphia, Pennsylvania. They both sounded a long ways away.

The Miners had visited Aunt Nora only once, that being at Thanksgiving, and they had brought Rodney along. Steven didn't recognize him. All the 'baby fat' was of course gone since he was a bit older, but Steven didn't expect him to be so thin. He had changed much over the years and was very quiet. When Steven ran to hug his little brother, Rodney pulled back in fear. Steven patted him on the shoulder instead, and Rodney tried to smile, his eyes darting about more as a caged animal. Steven didn't think Rodney remembered him as his brother at all, but he was careful to write down the Miners address anyway, in hopes of exchanging letters.

The farm was becoming intolerable for Steven. George's ranting and his bouts with his sanity had steadily grown worse and yet Aunt Nora refused to accept the fact that he needed help. Steven had brought home a couple of letters from the mail box which he knew came from the army, but Aunt Nora would grow angry and throw the letters away. He could hear her muttering something about "follow-up examination, my foot. Like I can't take care of my own boy," and she would be in a bad temper the remainder of the day.

Aunt Nora tried to hide the truth from others as to George's outrageous behavior. Steven never knew what fit of temper George might show next and so began to close the trap door leading into the loft before he lay down to sleep at night. He would carefully place a heavy item on the door to prevent George from trying to get to him as he slept. This way, he could rest more comfortably knowing he would at least have some warning.

I feel that I must get away. I just know something bad is going to happen.

These were the words Steven had written to Randolph. His correspondence with his older brother was all that kept Steven going this last year as he dealt with the heavy work load and George's unpredictable tantrums. Randolph felt he knew his brother well through their many letters and accepted his words as truth. Randolph replied by sending Steven a bus ticket.

The ticket didn't show a date but reading the fine print, Steven knew he needed to use the ticket within the next sixty days. The ticket would take Steven from Abingdon all the way to High Point, North Carolina. Steven knew this ticket would be his salvation. He began to plan. But first he would need to be sure the ticket was hidden safely from George and that snoop, Frances. Aunt Nora had stopped climbing into the loft years ago, but he didn't trust the other two. And he would have to plan carefully to get some of his clothes out of the house.

"What did your brother have to say?" It was Frances asking and Steven felt a moment of panic, as if she knew.

"Nothing much. Just that he's working hard and he says his foreman is leaving and he might get his job." Steven told her.

Randolph had said that his foreman was leaving, but that was all. Steven added the extra bit to test Frances. He hoped she had not steamed open his letter before he got it. He prayed she didn't know about the ticket.

"Well, that'll be good. Foremen make more money."

Steven signed with relief. She wouldn't have missed a chance to catch him in a lie, so she had not opened the letter after all.

"What about your letter? I saw a letter came from Dottie today. Did she ask about me?" Steven hoped to change the subject from his own mail.

"As a matter of fact, she did. She said to tell Steven hello. That was about all."

"Does she plan to come here for a visit soon?" asked Steven

"Now you know she can't travel with that new baby. It'll be awhile, but I expect she'll make it by Christmas."

Steven knew he would be gone by then and would be sorry to miss her. He had always liked Dottie and while he rejoiced for her when she married and moved away with such a fine husband, he knew he had lost just another good part of his already shallow life. But he wouldn't miss being here for Christmas. The memories of Christmas were only cause for more sadness.

But he would not give himself away, and so only replied, "I'll be glad to see her."

CHAPTER 11

Joe had been back to Aunt Nora's many times, splitting wood, helping to stack hay, and cutting and hanging tobacco. Aunt Nora paid Joe a small wage when he helped with the tobacco, but Steven knew it was not the same rate she paid the white help. He tried to equalize the pay by taking additional food to Joe's house. Slipping extra food for Joe's family was only one reason Steven went by the house. He liked the boys, Joe Jr. and Danny. Steven kept his friendship secret from Aunt Nora, but the truth was that except for his brother Will, they were his favorite chums.

Joe promised to come back one day to teach Steven how to make a good box trap for rabbits. Steven had struggled on his own, and knew something just wasn't exactly right. Joe promised to help.

"You ready to go to work?" Joe asked, as he approached Steven.

Steven brought out his own box trap for Joe's inspection. Joe could see the many flaws in his workmanship, but wouldn't dash the boy's enthusiasm.

"Look's like you been workin' real hard, Steven. Not many could have figured this out on their own." Joe praised.

"Well, I kinda remember how Harold built one once. But it don't seem to work. The rabbits get the bait every time, but most times the trap don't get them."

The two bent their heads to the task under the disapproving eyes of Aunt Nora. She didn't like Steven being friends with Joe, but kept her silence. George on the other hand felt no restriction to be civil and chastised Steven often. Joe and Steven worked for an hour or so until Joe felt the rabbit trap was one worthy of catching the biggest and best rabbit in Washington County. They stood back to admire their work.

"You got you a fine lookin' trap there, Steven. Put some food on the table....your Aunt Nora can't find no fault in that." Joe reassured him.

55

Steven desperately wanted to tell Joe about the bus ticket he had hidden in the barn. He had picked out a good hiding place, one he thought neither George or nosey Frances would find, and he was adding a few clothes and personal items. Some mornings, before going out to do his chores, Steven would put on an extra shirt or a pair of trousers under his work clothes. He didn't own many, most of them just old, ill-fitting hand-me-downs of George's which Aunt Nora had made a half-hearted attempt to alter. But he figured he better take all of them if he could, least ways the best ones, the ones that sorta fit.   After reaching the barn, he would remove the extra clothing and put the item in his secret place so that when the time was right he could take his ticket, his clothes and the few possessions he owned and make his getaway. He thought within the next month he would be ready to do just that.

But he didn't tell Joe. He was afraid Joe might try to talk him out of it. And Steven knew he had to get away.

CHAPTER 12

It was about two weeks after he and Joe built the rabbit trap that Aunt Nora and Frances had their regular monthly Missionary Meeting at church. Steven heard the men at church talking after services one Sunday and according to them this meeting was thirty minutes missionary followed by two hours of gossip. Steven knew he would have some time to himself without their usual watchful eyes, and could sort through his meager belongings to decide what he needed to take when he left the farm. He also needed to take some sort of valise or toting sack out to the barn so he would have a suitable carrying device for his trip.

Steven was returning from the barn, adding to his get-away stash, when he was met by George. George wore a vicious grin on his face and Steven knew things were going to get ugly.

"Guess what I been a doin'?" George said softly but with a voice filled with malice.

"Aunt Nora will be home any minute now," Steven warned him.

"No she won't. She said she wouldn't be home near on supper time." George said.

"Well, I got chores to do." Steven said this as he tried to push his way pass George's large frame.

"Got somethin' to show ya first." George said. He tried to make his voice sound enticing, but it didn't fool Steven.

George went several feet toward the orchard and pointed to the ground. There lay Steven's new rabbit trap, or what was left of it. It had been viciously stomped into dozens of small splintered pieces.

"Why'd you go and do that?" Steven cried. But in his heart, Steven knew why. It was the sort of thing the cruel guards would have done to George during his incarceration. Sometimes on his darkest days, George couldn't differentiate between his sadistic captors and himself. Aunt Nora had explained he was acting out his fears, only he didn't know just who he really was. Steven couldn't

57

say he truly understood all of that, but he did know it scared him plenty.

"Poor little cry baby. Maybe I'll just stomp you next."

Steven ran. He had no particular direction in mind, only to get away and stay out of sight until Aunt Nora came home. He couldn't leave. His clothes, and more important his bus ticket were in the barn and George was between him and the barn. No, he would just have to hide out. So he ran as fast as he could. Steven topped a rise and tumbled into a ravine. He waited breathlessly but didn't hear any sound and felt he had outrun George and would be safe to wait there for a couple of hours. He was breathing hard, as much from fear as from the run. The weather was warm so Steven stretched out in the sun for his long afternoon wait.

"Thought you'd get away from me? I was trained with the army's best, little boy. I can track you down." George voice coming from behind Steven almost scared him into a stand still shock, but not quite. Off he took running again with George in hot pursuit. Steven reached an old gravel pit and began to climb up the side. He hoped his youthfulness might help him in this situation. George had taken on some weight and maybe wasn't quite as agile.

"Go away. Go away, George. I think I hear Aunt Nora calling you." Steven yelled, hoping to trick him.

"Ain't nobody callin' me," was George's only response.

Steven climbed even higher onto the rocks and as he stepped up onto a shelf, the rocks moved beneath his feet. He grabbed hold of a ledge with both hands and held on fast. The rocks were tumbling down in great force, big rocks and small rocks, taking more with them. Steven heard a loud scream. As he pulled himself safely upon the ledge, he looked down at the bottom of the gravel pit and saw George lying there. He wasn't moving. There seemed to be some blood on his face, just above the right eye. Steven watched in horror, thinking George would get up at any minute and come after him again.

But George wasn't moving.

"Oh, Lordy, Lordy, I've killed him. I've killed him," Steven screamed these words over and over.

He didn't know what to do. They would arrest him and he didn't mean to do it. It was an accident. He was only trying to get away. Aunt Nora wouldn't have him now, she wouldn't want nothin' to do with somebody who'd killed her George. Slowly Steven resumed his climbing and after reaching the top he took the long way home. He didn't want to look back at George's body.

CHAPTER 13

I am going away. Steven

That was all the note said. Steven left it on the kitchen table for his Aunt Nora. He had returned to the house, left his short note and then retrieved his clothing from the barn and put his bus ticket in his pants pocket. He would have just time enough to be out of sight before he passed his aunt and Frances returning home. He couldn't go to Will's, it was a long way to walk and even if he made it there before being found out, that'd be the first place they'd look. And so Steven headed for the home of one he considered to be his best friend.

"You done what?" Joe asked, unbelieving.

"I killed George. I didn't mean to, I swear to God I didn't. You gotta believe me." Steven was sobbing his heart out and Joe did believe him. He had never heard Steven swear in all his years, and knew it was a sacred oath to him. Joe just didn't know what to do now.

"Then we'll just explain it to the sheriff. They don't lock you up for accidents. Least not white folk. Least not a young boy like yourself," Joe reasoned.

"I can't go back. Aunt Nora didn't like having me there in the first place, now she'll just hate me more," Steven pleaded.

"Steven, you're welcome to stay with me, but I got a wife and two youngins' to think of. What if the sheriff think we did do somethin' wrong? Maybe even that I was there and now we tryin' to hide it? I love you, boy, but I got to think of my family." Joe paced as he spoke, clearly torn between shielding the boy and risking his own.

"Please, Joe, just until I can figure out a way to get to Abingdon," Steven begged.

"What's Abingdon got to do with it?"

"I got a bus ticket. My brother sent it to me. And I left a note on the kitchen table so Aunt Nora wouldn't go looking for me," Steven explained.

61

"All right then. That's a bit differen'. Maybe we can work this out. You stay here til dark. Then I'll get my oldest, Joe Jr., to drive you to Abingdon......that is if you don't mind riding in a wagon pulled by a mule. Ain't got an automobile, you know. But I ain't apologizin' for that. Took me a long time to save up for that mule."

"Thanks, Joe," he said gratefully.

"You got to hide in that wagon, hear? Don't want my boy to get mixed up in any questions from the sheriff." Joe continued to pace and to study the situation.

"There's no reason for anyone to think I was even there when George died. Maybe they'll just think he was out walking. I didn't hit him you know. It was all those rocks. And he was laying in a big pile of them."

"That's what I'm counting on," Joe said. "All the same, you leavin' on the same day has got to look like a mighty big coincidence. Might be questions asked. So me and my boys, we don't want to bring no attention to ourselves."

"I understand that, Joe." Steven was relieved to know he would soon be on his way. Hopefully he would board that bus and be on the road before anyone found George's body.

Joe and Steven went into the house, Joe cautioning him against saying anything to upset his wife, Lelia. But Joe needn't have worried. Steven didn't want to think or talk about the tragedy. Lelia called to them to wash up for supper. She had a big spread of collards, fried potatoes and cornbread. The five of them sat down just as they had done many times before. Lelia noted that neither Joe or Steven had much of an appetite, but kept her thoughts to herself.

"Joe, Jr., I need you to drive the wagon into town soon as you finish your supper," Joe told him. Joe Jr. looked at his father with shock showing on his face. This was not a normal request, but Joe Jr. had sensed something wrong and was ready to obey his father.

"Can I go too?" asked Danny.

"No. Well, wait, maybe that would be a good idea after all. Yes, if your momma don't mind, you can ride along too."

Just after dusk, with Joe Jr. at the reins and Danny sitting proudly by his side, the old wagon began its trip to Abingdon. Out of sight was a very frightened young man hidden in back. As Steven lay quietly under the blankets, he remembered that first day he had left the depot in Abingdon to come to the Carterson farm.   Young and separated from his family, he had thought that trip was frightening, he didn't know he would be leaving and having the same thoughts.

"I want to take the next bus that's going to High Point, North Carolina," Steven told the attendant when finally they reached their destination.   Joe Jr. had let Steven off at one of the darkest side streets and Steven had followed the lights to the Greyhound bus station.

"Got to go by way of Asheville, and change buses there. Same bus that's goin' to Winston-Salem goes to High Point. Just ask 'em when you get to the station." The bored attendant stamped Steven's ticket without looking up.   The attendant felt working at the bus ticket counter beneath his capabilities and avoided conversations with the travelers who passed through.   That suited Steven just fine.

"What time does the bus leave?" Steven asked.

"Quarter to nine." And with that the attendant walked away and resumed reading his book.   Steven took a seat as far away from the others as possible and tried to keep his face turned away.   He didn't want anyone to remember him being there, just in case the law came looking.   Since Lelia had given him supper he wasn't hungry at present, and tightly clutched his paper sack full of food she had sent along.   He had no money and this might just be all he would have to eat for a spell.   He didn't know how far he might have to walk to find his brother once he reached High Point.

Steven was very tired, whether from exhaustion or sheer nerves, and was dozing when the bus pulled into the station. He was the first passenger to climb aboard and passed several empty seats to find one near the back.   He carried his bag of clothes on board with him, and slid it beneath his seat, holding his paper sack with the food on his lap. It seemed much too long before the others got on board and settled in for the long bus ride over the curving mountain roads leading to Asheville.   Steven let out a long sigh when he felt the bus begin to move.   He looked out at the streets of Abingdon.   They were deserted, with only a few men standing in front of the Belmont

63

Hotel.   Perhaps they had just gotten in on the train, the Belmont being the most popular hotel in town due to its close proximity to the railway station.

Steven felt a rush of relief as the town fell further and further behind, and while he didn't think he could ever sleep peacefully again, he fell into deep slumber.   Before many hours passed they were pulling into the tiny bus station in Asheville.   The bus to High Point was not due until morning, so Steven went to the men's room.   He tried dampening his hair and pushing it back, but its usual unruliness prevailed.   He sat down to wait, and opened his sack of food.   The first thing he saw on top was a note, written painstakingly in pencil.

Rite to me soon as you settled so I know you alright.   You wil remember how to back the envlope so I get it.   Best to put your own adress inside so anybody look they don't see.   I will rite how things turn out.

Joe had not signed the note.   After tucking the note carefully in his pocket, Steven returned to his sack of food.

Knowing he needed to make it last as long as possible, he gently lifted out only one biscuit.   Lelia had opened the biscuit and smeared the center with some of her own blackberry jelly.   Steven ate it slowly, lingering over its taste.   He licked the traces of jelly from his fingers.   He had plenty of time to think about things before the bus arrived, too much time.   But eventually he was on his way again, this time the next stop would be his destination, High Point, North Carolina.

CHAPTER 14

"Do you know where Maple Street is?" Steven asked a man who was busily mopping the floor. The bus had pulled into High Point several minutes ago and after a hasty trip to the men's room, Steven was now ready to set about finding his brother. He knew from the address Randolph had a room rented in a boarding house on Maple Street. They had planned that Randolph would meet him at the bus station, and therefore no directions had been necessary before, but events changed all that. Now Steven would have to find that boarding house on his own.

He feared he might have to walk for quite some distance and time, but found the street he was looking for was only about ten blocks from where he now stood. Of course, Steven didn't understand what a 'block' was, but he figured it out real quick. Carefully following the directions, he walked along the unfamiliar streets. Once in a while a dog would follow along, sometimes a boy on a bike or a scooter, but mostly he was by himself. He had eaten another of Lelia's biscuits before the bus pulled into High Point but was feeling hungry once again. He'd find the boarding house first, then he would eat his last bit. The further he walked, the more dilapidated the houses looked. When he reached Maple Street he was surprised at how run down everything looked. At long last he stopped in front of a house that bore the same number Steven used on his mail to Randolph. This had to be the place. Nervously, he knocked on the door.

"Got no more rooms to rent. I'm full up." The woman who answered the door didn't look as if she meant to be rude, she was just tired and had no time for strangers. Her faded house dress was wrinkled and she wore only soiled house shoes on her feet. The sides were worn through and the tips of her toes were showing. She started to close the door, but Steven spoke up quickly.

"Ma'am. Please ma'am. I'm lookin' for my brother. I rode all the way from Virginia on a bus and I'm real anxious to find him," Steven pleaded.

"Well," the woman hesitated, "what's you name?" She knew that things weren't going all that good at some of the factories and a few folks had been laid off work. She wasn't going to be made a fool of by someone looking for a handout.

"Steven. I'm Randolph's brother. I been sending his mail to this address. It was him that sent me the ticket." Steven's words were spilling over one another in his anxiety to be sure this woman understood.

"Well, gracious me, I reckon I do see the family resemblance. He's been tellin' how you was a comin' soon." With that she threw open the door. "But your brother don't get off work for a couple more hours. I reckon you can wait in his room. He's told me all about you, Steven. Says you are a good boy. Pleased to meet ya."

"I'm pleased to meet you too, ma'am." Steven said with relief. She would never know just how relieved he felt. This whole thing had turned out better than he could ever have hoped. At Steven's embarrassed request, the woman showed Steven the privy out back and then up to Randolph's room. He was so exhausted he fell across the bed and remained there until he heard footsteps running up the stairs. The door burst open and there stood his brother. Randolph. At last.

"Steven! I'm plumb happy to see you, little brother, but I thought you'd write to me and tell me when you was comin'. I would 'a met you at the bus station."

Steven was amused to hear Randolph's drawl. After years with the loggers and now with the blue collar workers in the furniture factory, Randolph had picked up the sound and the slow speech mannerisms of the south. His voice was music to Steven's ears.

"I couldn't, Randolph. Something happened." And so with great trepidation but allowing no excuses for his own part, Steven spilled out the whole story. Randolph was first shocked, then angry, but most of all protective of his brother.

"I know Aunt Nora is a cold woman, and you're probably 'rite that she would have threw you out of the house anyway. I'm not sayin' it was your fault, it's just that she ain't gonna blame George on any part of it."

"What do I do now?" asked Steven.

"First, we talk to Mrs. Stone and get permission for you to stay here with me. She'll charge us a few dollars 'xtra, but that won't be a problem. We'll go looking for work for you t'morrow so you'll be bringing in a bit of pay."

Randolph had already been working on this prior to Steven's arrival. His foreman couldn't take on an extra man, things were too tight and the company was even laying off, but they did need a hand to do some janitorial work two days a week. If his brother was willing to do some sweeping and other heavier cleaning, they told Randolph, he could have the work. The pay was ten cents an hour, ten hour shifts. Randolph had already accepted on his brother's behalf.

CHAPTER 15

Joe was anxious to get into work next morning after his boys had seen Steven safely to Abingdon. Joe's one day a week job at the Merriman Produce House in Meadowview would allow him the opportunity to find out what, if anything, the folks around knew about George. He got to work a bit early, as was his practice, but none of the other men had much to say for the first couple of hours.   Joe loaded the chickens and the eggs onto the trucks in silence. Maybe they hadn't found the body yet, he thought. But surely George's momma would have the whole county out searching by this time.

"Hey fellars, did ye hear about ole crazy George Carterson?" a local yelled as he rushed into the produce warehouse. All the men stopped in rapt attention.

"He done gone and got hisself drowned," the man continued.

"Drown, did you say drown?" Joe asked.

"Yeah, I said 'drowned,' can't you hear?" the man said nastily. He wasn't addressing his remarks to Joe and didn't appreciate him interrupting his story.

"Old Missrus Carterson sent Frances in to fetch the sheriff last night about nine, maybe nine-thirty.   Said that youngin' had run off and she feared George had gone to search for him.   George never came back to the house." The local gossip was enjoying his moment of glory with all eyes and ears turned his way.

"What about the boy?" Joe asked.   He knew he was riling the bigot, but his desire to know overcame his caution at being the only colored man working with the white crew.

"What about the boy? The boy ain't drowned. It's ole George. I 'pect the boy just got tired of doing all the dirty work and runned off.   Least wise they didn't find no boy, but they found George a floatin' in that pond down near the Hyter's place."

Joe couldn't figure how this could be.   Steven said he had left George, apparently dead, but maybe now it wasn't so, at the rock quarry.   The pond had to be at least a half mile away.

69

The rocks must have knocked George out for a few minutes, Joe thought. On thinking back, Steven never went near the body. George wasn't dead, he only appeared so. *Good thing the boy ran,* he told himself, *George would have come to plenty mad. Might have done the boy real harm. But still, George must have been a mite dizzy from the blow on the head to have drown that way.* Joe knew that pond to be no more than waist deep and hoped someone would ask more questions. They did.

"Shucks, how in thunder could George drown in the pond? Ain't deep enough" one of Joe's co-workers protested.

"Don't know fer sure, but he's drowned alright. And old lady Carterson's a carryin' on somethin' fierce."

"Might be George just got all turned around......in the dark 'n all," one of the men said.

"'Speck so. Onlyest way I can figur'," another said, thought-fully.

The workers were silence for a few minutes, letting this news sink in. Finally one of them stroked his chin and mused, "Well, if'en George was after that boy, I'd say he weren't after him to bring him back home outta thinkin' kindly of him. You fellers know George ain't been right since he got back from that POW camp. I know them Carterson's is too proud to let on, but George done got mean. Might be that's why the boy took off."

"Yeah, it jest might be," agreed another.

The talk went on for several minutes while Joe did his best to hang around within hearing distance but not to show too much interest. So far nothing they said implicated Steven as having anything to do with the death, only that he might have been running away from George. Which after all was the truth, but Joe would keep his silence on that matter.

Throughout the day workers on their lunch break and drifters with no place special to go would stop by the produce warehouse to talk over the drowning death of one of their citizens. All seemed of one opinion. George had come back from the war a different man, a fact they could all feel sorry about. The boy had most likely been trying to escape a harsh life made worse by George's insanity, but no

70

one related the drowning as being an act of violence.   George was big and strong.   Steven was a boy.   No one saw the drowning as anything but an accident.   Joe hoped the day would come that he could share this news with Steven.

Joe had almost finished loading the last truck when the foreman approached him.

"Joe!   Mrs. Merriman wants to see you at her house 'fore you go home," he told him.

"Yes, suh." Joe answered, head bowed.

CHAPTER 16

The Merrimans owned most of the stores in Meadowview. There was the produce house, where Joe worked at least one day a week, a feed store and a combination mercantile and grocery store. They were a respected family and fair to their employees. Joe had met Mrs. Merriman on several occasions and found her to be a nice lady. So as requested, Joe stopped by her house before going home. He walked up on the big veranda at the back of the house and politely knocked on the door. Their maid answered and asked Joe to wait while she let Mrs. Merriman know he was there. Joe waited, hat in hand.

"Joe, thank you for stopping by." Mrs. Merriman greeted him. She had this wonderful way about her of not talking down to the hired help, but spoke to them as if they were friends. Joe liked her for that. "I wanted to ask if you could help me do some clearing out tomorrow. I've so many old things stored away, and my husband is insisting I sort through some of the 'junk' as he likes to call it and get it hauled away." Her voice was merry and she tilted her head to one side as she waited for Joe's answer. She was a petite woman, in her mid-fifties, slightly plump, with brown hair beginning to show streaks of gray.

"I'd be happy to, ma'am," Joe told her politely. He didn't have to grovel and act ignorant in front of Mrs. Merriman, but at the same time he knew 'his place' as it were and didn't make any assumptions. He would respect her kindness to him. And he was happy to do this job. His one day a week at the produce warehouse gave him some pocket money week-to-week, but he liked picking up extra work whenever possible. And he knew Mrs. Merriman to be fair in her pay. He didn't even ask what that might be.

The next morning when Joe arrived at Mrs. Merriman's residence to begin helping her with her clearing out, he had no way of knowing that this day would change the fate of one of his children; his youngest son, Danny. Joe worked well into the morning, doing the lifting and carrying, Mrs. Merriman giving the commands. At

73

lunch time they paused and she had a sandwich and a cold glass of lemonade sent out for Joe.

She is nice like that, Joe thought, *not like some of the places I've worked all day without rest or food. She's a fine lady.*

By mid-afternoon, Mrs. Merriman, with Joe's help, had cleared most of the heavy items from the garage and storage area. In the back, against the wall, there was a large item covered with a blue tarpaulin. Joe removed the tarpaulin to discover an old upright piano. He ran his fingers over the keys. Some sounded out of tune, even to him who knew nothing about music.

"This old piano was my first. I learned to play on it." Mrs. Merriman explained. "I've always hated the thought of getting rid of it."

"I understand," Joe said. "My Danny, that be my youngest one, he's musical. Anything to do with music, well to him it's sort of sacred. He would understand you not wantin' to part with it."

"I didn't know you had a son who played music," she answered.

"Oh, yes'm. We, that is my wife Lelia and me, we didn't know it either at the first. My Lelia, she cleans for the Pattersons, maybe you know them, over near Cedarville. They been letting Lelia bring Danny along on her cleanin' days since he was a little thing. He stay outside or in the laundry room and play. He a real good boy. Now Mrs. Patterson, she got one of them big Victrola's, I believe they call. And Mrs. Patterson, she play music all the time my Lelia say. She even sent away to New York for most of it. My Danny would sit outside the window when the weather be good and he listen for as long as Mrs. Patterson would crank that machine."

It was the longest speech Joe had ever made before a white lady and he felt he may have overstepped his bounds in his enthusiasm. "How sweet," she said. Mrs. Merriman had clearly lost interest.

"We knew he like music, so for Christmas one year we got him a harmonica. He started playin' the prettiest music you ever hear. My Lelia say it be the same music he hear at Mrs. Patterson's house.

74

"That's remarkable." Perhaps she was a bit more interested in this line of conversation than she first thought.

"And then," Joe continued, not willing to stop his tale, "a few months later we was havin' a deacons meetin' after preachin' and the family had to wait a spell for me. Danny, he sneaked back in church, and he was playin' the same music on the church piano. Course at first, he was just pickin' out the tune with one finger. But it weren't long till he was playin' real."

"Just playing by ear?" she asked.

"I think that's how they 'splained it, ma'am. He can play anythin' he hear."

"What does he play, gospel? You say he heard the music at the Patterson's? What kind of music?" She was becoming more and more intrigued by this story.

"I don't have an ear for music, ma'am. But my Lelia, she say it what Mrs. Patterson call 'classical.' It's music I hear folk like Mrs. Patterson put great stock in. They got funny names. One is somebody sound like Show Pan and then there's another one they call Bait,.......Bait... Something. Can't remember the rest of it." Joe shook his head.

"Are you telling me that your son can play Beethoven on the piano?" Mrs. Merriman clearly didn't believe this.

"Yes'm. That's it. Bait-hoven. That's a funny name, ma'am, but that's what they call him alright. Yes'm."

"And he plays well?"

"You mean my Danny or this Baithoven feller?" Joe was pretty sure she meant Danny but thought it wise to be sure.

"Danny, of course. Does he play well?"

"I can't say, ma'am. I never heard this music he's a playin' so I got nothing to compare it to. Course his momma, she say he good. But then Danny, he fuss. He say his fingers not long enough to reach across all the keys like they 'spose to." Joe laughed as he thought of Danny's little red face when he would grow frustrated at the sound he wanted, but couldn't attain.

"Where does he play now? Does he still play at the church?"

"Yes'm. Oncet our preacher saw Danny was playin' serious

75

and not foolin' around, he lets him come in the church two, three times a week. But they struck a deal. Danny got to play the 'Lord's music' for the first 30 minutes, then he can play his 'classical' music." Joe explained.

Mrs. Merriman spent several moments in thought. The nearby college, Emory & Henry, which she and her husband supported financially, had just hired a new music professor. She had wanted to have a little reception for him. If there really were a young Negro boy of her acquaintance who could actually play these classical numbers, what a coup it would be for her to present him as her surprise entertainment for the evening. Even if he were a little amateur, it would still be a great surprise! But first, she wanted to hear this boy for herself. She wouldn't dare chance an embarrassment, she would audition the boy first.

"Joe, do you think that your son, what did you say his name was, would come over and play something for me before we move this piano away? I realize it is most likely out of tune, but it would give me a chance to hear him."

"His name is Danny, ma'am. And I'd say he would probably play anywhere. He love to play, but he don't get much practice as he want. He surely wants to play every single day."

"Ask him if he will come and play for me. If he plays as well as you've led me to believe, I will gladly have this old piano tuned and it's his to keep. I really do need to get it moved to make space, and I'd love to see it go to someone who would love it. But no promises, understand? I need to hear just what he can do."

"Yes, ma'am!"

"And Joe, ask Danny to pick out about two of his favorite 'Lord's music.' I'd like to hear some of those too."

"I'll tell him, ma'am. And thank you. Thank you. I'll ask our preacher if he'll let Danny practice some extra 'fore he come. I know Danny be terrible nervous, playin' for you. But onct he get to playin', he forget evrythin' and he not nervous no more. Just give him a few minutes, if you please."

"Joe, I want the boy to succeed. I will absolutely listen with an open mind. I don't expect him to be perfect." Mrs. Merriman

76

answered. She didn't know if the boy was any good, but if he were it would certainly give cause for her evening's entertainment to be the talk of the town. Yes, she absolutely wanted him to succeed. In fact, she'd call the piano tuner first thing in the morning. If she was going to give the piano to anyone, Danny or anyone else, it needed to be in good condition, right? A young Negro boy who could play Beethoven. No one would believe her find if it were true.

Joe didn't remember walking home that night. His feet never touched the ground. He might have seen a miracle today. He had worried and grieved over not being able to get a piano for Danny. He knew the boy had 'the gift.' But now that piano was in their grasp. If Danny played good enough for Mrs. Merriman, and he knew his boy could do it, Danny was going to have his own piano.

Joe had already forgotten all about George Carterson.

CHAPTER 17

After Steven's arrival, Randolph sent off a letter to both Will and Susan. He didn't want them to worry if they should hear that Steven had left the Carterson farm. He also strongly urged them to the keep Steven's whereabouts to themselves. He didn't give a reason. No mention was made of George.

Susan's response was brief but expressed her joy that the two brothers were together, Will's letter was a little longer. He had been concerned about Steven, but thought he would be hearing soon. He told Randolph of his trip to visit Rodney and how disappointed he had been with the visit. Rodney had been very withdrawn and did not seem to be "warming up" to his brother. No mention was made of George.

Steven and Randolph fell into a routine which was to last for nearly two years. While Randolph had to work six days when the work was available, Steven worked only two regular, but volunteering for extra hours every chance he got. On his off days, Steven would do their laundry and anything else that needed doing. Mrs. Stone allowed the boys to keep a hot plate in their room for an extra dollar a week. Sometimes Steven tried his hand at cooking. It wasn't much, but it saved a bit on things to pack for their lunches. He tried to keep the room clean, Mrs. Stone supplying clean sheets every two weeks.

A long time has passed since that night Steven fled to the bus station and he felt he now had the courage to find out what, if any, trouble he might be in. He wrote to Joe. He dreaded doing it, but hoped enough time had elapsed and folks had forgotten about him. He felt reasonably safe since no one had traced him to High Point and trusted Joe with his address, but did practice caution as Joe had advised and put his return address inside the envelope.

Within a fortnight he received a reply. He recognized Joe's penciled scrawl on the envelope.

Stevie boy, Joe had written, *don't worry none bout what*

happenin' here.   You was not the one hurt your cusin George. The rocks just nocked him cold but he come to. They found him dead but not cause of anything you done. He in the pond   the one over at Hyter place and he was drowned.   Don't know how he get there but your Aunt Nora say he must have found you note and went looking. She try to make him hero.   Guess he be looking alright   but not for reson she try to say. You done rite to leave. We miss you boy and the wife   and the boys say they hope you doing good and come see us when you can.   Your friend.

Only a person who has suffered from guilt and fear could know the relief that flooded through Steven when he read those words. George's death might still be associated with his leaving, and in a way it was, but the blame had not been put on Steven as being the one who had harmed him.   There might even be a few folks back in Virginia who saw through it all and felt George's motives in 'searching' for Steven was not for a good purpose.   But that didn't matter now, it was over. Let sleeping dogs lie.

Just as Steven thought that life could go on as it was, world events were about to change his life.   The foreman sadly informed Steven they could no longer keep him on. It was the year 1929, and the banks were closing their doors leaving many penniless. Money was scarce. Too many of the men had lost their jobs and even two days of work looked good to them. The factory management would have to offer even a few hours work to their older employees as long as they could.   Added to this, Randolph was reduced to three days a week with a gentle warning that this too might end soon. The two brothers knew this would not be enough to support them and they talked long into the night as to what they might do now.

Early next morning, Steven made a long walk into the countryside looking for farmland. He came upon one farmer putting out hay for his cattle. Steven stopped and asked for work. The farmer could sorely use some help, but had no way to pay the young man.

"Do you have any extra vegetables or fruit? At this time of year you might have turnips, fall cabbage or apples? Did your wife put away canned goods? Corn? Tomatoes? That will be all the pay I need." And so they struck a deal.

80

Next day, Steven set up a box on a busy corner downtown and sold the turnips and apples, three for a penny. It wasn't much but it was the best he could do. Just five of those pennies would buy a loaf of bread to take back to his and Randolph's room. The canned goods he kept. So Steven began his new 'career' as farmer's helper one day, vegetable vender the next. The farmer's wife had many jars of canned goods of cherries, pickles, green beans, along with assorted jams and jellies. There were many more than she and her husband could eat, and besides she knew they would be growing another garden in the spring. Steven sold the excess at a low price and split the money with the farmer's wife. This plan worked well until the late fall and winter was setting in.

Christmas was dismal that year, but they made their little paper chains like their mother had taught them and put up a tiny cedar tree in their room. On Christmas morning, Steven gave Randolph a special whistle he had carved and Randolph gave Steven a small wooden case to hold his 'valuables' he said. He had made it from scraps from the furniture factory. It was the best gift Steven could remember ever receiving. Here he was, going on nineteen when most considered that a grown man, and he felt his eyes filling. He turned away, embarrassed, not knowing that the emotion made it all the more special to Randolph.

"We'll get through the winter somehow," Randolph worried. "I just don't know what to do. I feel guilty about bringing you here with no future."

"I got family. That's the best thing that ever happened to me." Steven didn't know how to tell Randolph what these last two years had meant to him. They had so little, many times going hungry and now faced with a harsh winter, but he wouldn't have traded it for anything.

"I been writing to Harold, did you know that?" Randolph asked one day.

"Why did you keep it a secret?"

"I didn't know what he might be 'a doin', if he even remembered us. I didn't want to git your hopes up."

"My hopes up about what?" Steven asked. He thought he

might see a plot here, and wondered what in the world Randolph was planning.

"He's in Detroit. I got his address from Aunt Martha back in Greeneville. I reckon she's the only'est one that's kept track of all of us."

"Is he coming back here?" asked Steven.

"I don't think so. Looks like he likes the big city. Guess he thinks we're still a bunch of country bumpkins, sort of like it was when he went away. Probably don't know things has changed here too."

"Well, then……..."

"He wants us to come up there. To Detroit." Randolph answered.

"Are you goin'?" Steven asked. It really didn't matter to him, one way or the other. Despite all the hardships, he had been really happy here with Randolph but would change things if Randolph said so.

"I was thinkin' we might ought to go, but only one at a time. Truth is, I don't think we can come up with more'n one ticket. So it makes sense for you to go first. See, I got sometimes as much as two, three days o' work coming to me, while you got none right now. So I'll just hang on and let you go and git work, then you and Harold send me the money so's I can come too." Randolph seemed to have it all worked out and there was no hesitation in his voice. Steven believed in his plan.

The next morning the two brothers wrote a letter to Harold, accepting his invitation to come to Detroit. They thought it a good plan, such a big city, so much work going on. They would seal their futures and it would all come to a very happy ending. Steven agreed to go first.

"I don't like going without you, Randolph. It feels like leaving again. All the sadness comes back and I can't help but think of Papa and Momma."

"Don't even think on it, little brother. This is the last time we'll be apart. And it won't be for long. Wherever you are, that's where I'll be. You can count on it. Don't you think I need family too? I been wantin' it since that first day I went to the loggin' camp." Randolph hugged his brother, not caring if the other folks at the station found it amusing that the two big brothers were trying very hard to blink away the mist that filled their eyes. And so once again, Steven began a long tedious trip which he didn't want to take, but destiny demanded that he make.

CHAPTER 18

"Wake up! We're here. Everybody off," cried the conductor. He had rapped on Steven's feet to awaken him. The train ride, a luxury put together by all three of the brothers, had been so much better than a bus ride, but even so had taken many hours and Steven fell into a sleep of pure exhaustion. He awoke and stumbled to find his bag of clothing and few other personal possessions such as his hat and gloves. It was all he owned in this world.

Before departing the train he looked out the window at the station where they had just arrived. He was amazed at the size. It must be two, maybe three, four times the size of the station he had left in High Point. And there were so many people, where in the world were all these people going? The women looked real elegant. That was a word Frances used to say a lot, 'elegant.' Frances wouldn't have believed all the women with their big warm fur coats. They were nestled down inside them like it were part of their skin. But Steven had expected Detroit to be a bit colder than he was used to in the south so he thought fur coats just might be a necessity here. He stepped from the train.

"Steven!"

He heard the voice but didn't recognize it. He hadn't seen Harold in years. How could Harold know it was he? At once, a huge man with the build, hair and eyes of Papa, those Williams eyes, greeted him.

"Harold?" he asked.

"I'd a known you anywhere, Stevie. Who else has all that fly-away hair? You haven't changed a bit. Well, maybe a mite taller and filled out a bit, but the same ole Stevie." With that Harold grabbed his brother and hugged him as though he might never let go.

Once again Steven felt those darn tears coming up to cloud his vision. Would he never get past that? He would never have imagined it was going to be such a heartrending moment to see his

85

oldest brother again. He hadn't reflected much on Harold in the past few years, he thought, and he felt guilty over this fact. He was realizing that Harold had been very close to Steven's own age now when he first struck out on his own. He must have been just as frightened and unsure as Steven felt now, but Steven had an older brother to lean on. Harold would have had no one, but had seemed so very grown up at the time. Steven tried to straighten his shoulders and look Harold in the eye like a man. But his attempts failed and he ended up hugging his brother even tighter.

"You look just great," Harold said when he knew Steven had gained control of his emotions.

"You too," was all Steven could utter at the moment.

"Let's go home. Well, home might not be the right word for it, I have a small place for now. Just two rooms, but there's a bed and a couch so we got room for sleeping. And a tiny kitchen and two chairs. We're gonna do just fine. And when we can get Randolph up here too, we'll get a bigger place." Harold didn't mean to boast, but he needed Steven to look up to him as his older brother for just a bit. Later he knew that Steven would see through the bravado, but for now he needed the younger one's confidence.

"Whatever you say, Harold. I'm just looking to find work. I'll pay my own way."

The two brothers left the train station, carrying Steven's meager belongings between them. It was a long walk, but Steven was accustomed to walking and didn't ask any questions. They passed several stores which appeared to be small grocer's but some of the foods displayed were not familiar to Steven. The words printed on the windows along with the price seemed to indicate maybe these were foods from a different nationality. Steven tried to recall some of his lessons from school. He was pretty sure he could identify some of the words. They also passed some places that were boarded up, but folks were still going in through a small door. They seemed to know where they were going, although there were no signs. Lots of girls stood outside in the cold and even while the temperature was very low and Steven was extremely cold in his warmest clothes, these girls were scantily clad. They started to approach the two brothers until Randolph held up his hand and told them to go away. *Strange behavior,* thought Steven, *I wonder what they are doing here and why he doesn't want to say hello to them?*

As they approached Harold's apartment house, two strange looking men walked toward them.

"What you got there?" they asked Harold.

"None of your business," Harold replied as he kept walking, increasing his pace.

This was a puzzlement to Steven, not knowing why Harold would be rude to these people, and this the second time in only a few minutes. The men were dressed 'funny' according to Steven's experience with men's clothing. They wore suits, with two sets of buttons down each side of the coat, and they wore funny looking shoes, shiny, and had on strange hats. These clothes didn't fit into anything Steven had seen in High Point and certainly not in Abingdon. Steven had to assume this must be the dress of men in big northern cities and stared at them with open curiosity.

"Think on our offer?" one of the strange men asked.

"You go to the devil," was Harold's surprising answer. Steven held his questions to himself. If his brother didn't like these men, and it was so bad it led to swearing which his parents would never have permitted from any of them, then he guessed the men must be really bad and he wasn't going to like them either. But he couldn't help but wonder why Harold had such an adverse attitude toward them?

"Come on in," Harold said as they reached his small apartment. It was as if he had dismissed the men from his mind. Steven opted not to mention them.

"This is just the best, the finest....... I don't know what to say. I've spent the last years of my life except for the time with Randolph, living out of a loft. I can't believe how it must feel to have all this space to yourself." Steven spoke without thought. If he had taken time to think about it, he would have realized what it had taken Harold to achieve even this tiny space for himself......the loneliness, the struggles, the homesickness to see his siblings. Steven didn't realize how lucky he had been. He had Will close by, he had

87

seen Rodney once and Susan maybe three or four times, and then his time spent with Randolph. But Harold had no one. All of this had taken a very hard toll on Harold's peace of mind.

Next morning, Steven made all the rounds, looking for work. He went to huge factories with smoke billowing out of their tall stacks; he went to what he knew were called 'skyscrapers' where major construction companies had their offices, he walked until he felt he would drop. There were long lines of folks looking for work, everywhere. And a farm boy with no experience didn't stand a chance. Steven felt guilty when he came home each night and reported no luck. He felt he was not only letting Harold down, but also Randolph who was waiting back in High Point for word to join them. Harold would just pat his back and assure him things would get better tomorrow. There was always tomorrow.

***

"You ready yet?" It was the same funny dressed men whom Steven had seen the first day he arrived. They were once again questioning Harold and Steven had not even a clue as to what they wanted. Harold quickened his steps without answering them.

"What are they talking about?" Steven asked.

"They're racketeers. Just try to ignore them."

"Well, I've at least read about racketeers in the newspaper so I guess I know what you mean. But why are they talking to you?"

"Because they want me to come to work for them," Randolph answered.

"Doing what?" Steven asked. "I need work. Don't they have some businesses that are okay? Why don't you talk to them. Maybe they'll offer the job to me."

"No!" shouted Harold.

"Why not?"

"They want me to do what they call 'running numbers' for them. But that's only the beginning, Steven. I've seen a lot of my friends get involved with them. Once they've got you, they own you. You can never, ever leave them."

88

"Or what?"

"Or they kill you.   They don't leave witnesses to talk." Randolph answered with a defeated voice.

"But why you?" Steven asked.

"They think I have an 'honest face.' They say I've got that country twang in my voice that sounds like an honest person. Most of the men who work for them are city 'slickers' like the ones you see talking to me.   People are a little leery.....don't always trust them. They need a man who looks like a greenhorn, one that people will just naturally think too dumb to be dishonest, and they'll trust me. These men run a lot of scams, so the kind of person they want, well, they think that's me."

There was no further discussion on the subject, but Steven did see the same men trying to talk to Harold a few more times.   In the meantime he kept looking for work, but to no avail.

CHAPTER 19

The nation was in trouble, that was for sure. Steven hoped the year 1930 would bring good things, but it seemed more and more people were out of work. There was nothing to be found, not even in the big city of Detroit. Then one day Harold came home with bad news of his own.

"I've lost my job, Steven. Guess we'll have to delay sending for Randolph anytime soon," was all he had to say, but the struggle with which he said it told Steven he was much more upset than he wanted to show.

"We'll look together. Tomorrow is a new day." Steven tried to reassure him, not believing his own optimism.

The two brothers did look, for weeks. One day they saw a very long line forming and assuming it was leading to a company taking applications, they fell into place. When finally they turned a corner and could see the location they were waiting in line for, they saw it was a soup kitchen. With so many out of work, the city had set up soup kitchens around town to feed the many hungry. The brothers took a vote and decided to stay in line. They were rewarded with not only a huge bowl of good nourishing soup, but a small loaf of bread each. They devoured their prize with gusto.

Returning to the apartment, Harold took out a deck of cards and began to teach Steven how to play Gin Rummy. Aunt Nora had thought cards were the work of the devil and so Steven had never played before. He caught on quickly. It's amazing how much better you feel after a hot meal, and the boys were feeling the best they had in days. As they played, they talked.

"Where did you go when you first came to Detroit?" Steven asked him.

"I lived in the car. I didn't know where to go at first, so I just parked Papa's old car and slept there. I was looking for work and not finding any. I was getting pretty hungry and started searching behind some of the big restaurants for food. I found they throw out a lot of stuff that's not really that old. The manager caught me." Harold told him.

"What did he do? Did you get in trouble?   If they threw it out, that's not stealing," Steven protested.

"No, I didn't get in trouble.   It turned out to be a good thing. The man said if I wanted to pick up scraps, then I should come inside and clean off the tables and such.   He put me to work, washing dishes and things like that," Harold said.

"Was it bad?"

"No, not really. At least I got to eat for free, and they paid me a little bit, not much. But after a few days the man got to talking to me more, found out I graduated eighth grade. That was more education than most of the help there had, so they let me run the cash register.   That was better, but it still didn't pay much," Harold told him. "The car was about gone. All four tires were flat and I didn't have money to buy new ones.   So I sold it real cheap, but I was able to rent a room with the money."

"And then what happened?   I know you don't work at a restaurant now."

"No," he answered, "A lot of important men eat at that restaurant on a regular basis.   My boss, he knew I could do better and he was a good man, he introduced me to some of them and they told me to come around to their factory and fill out an application.   I got on at one of them."

"And then you moved here?" Steven asked.

"Not right away.   I still didn't have much money.   I had to eat out since all I had was a room and I couldn't eat free at the restaurant no more, and I had to pay somebody to wash my clothes.   It was hard savin' up." Harold explained.

"Did you ever think about coming back home? Or at least back to Virginia?" Steven asked him.

"No, least wise not more than once a day," Harold laughed.

"Then why?   Why didn't you come?" Steven wanted to know.

"Pride I guess.   I thought if I came back I'd end up on one of those farms as a laborer.   I just kept thinking any day things were going to get better, if I'd just hang on a bit." He shrugged his shoulders to imply he wasn't sure if it had been the right decision.

Weeks went by and no work was found. Harold was warned if he didn't pay his rent, he would be evicted from his apartment. He promised to do his best, and begged for more time. With so many out of work and no hope of renting to anyone in a better situation, the landlady agreed. Without telling Steven, Harold wrote to Randolph and told him of their plight. More weeks went by without finding work. Finally, Harold's resolve wore down. He accepted the job with the mob, the 'racketeers' as it were.

"But I have one request," he told them.

"You don't tell us your request. It works the other way around," they snarled at him.

"I want a train, no, make that a bus ticket for my brother. I want him to leave Detroit." Harold asked.

"That's the kid you always got wit 'cha?" they asked.

"Yes, I want him out of town."

"We want him out of town, too. He's still wet behind the ears, a greenie, guys like that just cause us trouble. We'll get him a ticket on the next train out. Where to?"

"He won't believe I came up with enough money for the train. Better make it bus fare. And make it to High Point, North Carolina." Harold told them.

Harold sent off a letter to Randolph to let him know that Steven would be returning. That was fine with Randolph, he was still holding on to two, three days a week of work and had found better and cheaper living quarters with a family further out in the country. He had met a girl he liked a lot, a girl named Faith, and didn't really want to leave just yet. Steven was welcome to join him and Randolph expressed his sorrow that the two of them had not been able to find work so they could all be together. Randolph noted how sad Harold had sounded. Gosh, he shouldn't be that sad. They'd tried, after all. He'd done his best.

****

93

And so Steven began his long journey back to North Carolina. He had liked being with Harold but the city wasn't where he really wanted to be. He begged Harold to come back with him, but Harold insisted he had some business to take care of first. Steven saw the sorrow in Harold's eyes and knew those men in their funny little suits and shoes had something to do with Harold's sudden decision to send him away.

Steven didn't know it would be the last time he would see his oldest brother. When word didn't come over a period of time, Steven tried to contact him. Others tried too, but to no avail. Had they been able to see the demise of their brother Harold they would have seen a remorseful and desperate man. He worked for the 'mob' in Detroit until one day he could take it no longer. So many people whose lives were ruined, so many killings. Harold had not pulled the trigger himself but he felt dirty, knowing he should have done something. He told his boss he was quitting, leaving Detroit altogether. The boss didn't let people quit. They knew too much. The next day workers found a body floating in the river. There was no identification on the body.

****

The landlady waited as long as she could. She'd liked her tenant, and thought he was a good decent man. So polite, with a slight southern drawl to his speech. Called her Ma'am, he did. Not like that riff-raff that came around some days. But money was tight and his room rent was well past due. She let herself in with her own key and began putting the man's belongings in bags. There was a letter on the table, addressed to some fellows in North Carolina. But there wasn't any stamp on the letter. She hesitated for a moment, not sure what she should do. But then with a shrug, she decided to just toss it out. Wasn't her responsibility to mail someone else's letter.

No one would ever read the words:

Dear Randolph and Steven:

I am planning to leave the city of Detroit behind and return to my southern roots...................................

94

CHAPTER 20

Steven finally found some work in North Carolina. It wasn't the work he would have wanted but that didn't really matter. He was accustomed to hard work and found many of the farmers in the North Carolina region were desperate for a good hand, but couldn't afford one. Most farmer's had had their sharecroppers in the past, but for now there wasn't enough money coming in to support one family, much less two, and so they were doing all the work themselves.

"Howdy, could you use a hand?" Steven would say, real friendly.

It was evident the men were having a hard time doing a two man job alone, and when Steven jumped into the work and showed his experience and know how, the men were obliged to offer him some small payment.

Steven was able to pick up enough work by rotating his services among ten or twelve different farmers to pay room and board and they threw in enough vegetables and fruit to keep he and his brother from being hungry. When Steven thought back to his last starving days in Detroit, he felt wealthy indeed. He was once again sharing a room with Randolph, and everything was back to normal.

Concerned for his brother Rodney, Steven felt compelled to write to him at the Miner's residence. He knew so little of Rodney, but he did vividly recall how Randolph had saved his skin and if Rodney needed some help, then it was his duty to pass the good deed along to his youngest brother. Steven's last letter from Will did not sound too promising for Rodney's life at the Miners. "*I paid Rodney a visit last week. He is so withdrawn, he doesn't seem to want to talk to me,*" Will had written. Reading between the lines he knew Will was worried, and so was he.

Steven's letter to Rodney was polite, not one that insinuated Rodney needed his intervention, but he tried to form the words that would let him know he was there for him if he ever needed his help. Steven's own life was so full right now, he didn't dwell on past sadness. He was just living for the present. Especially one thing in the present.

He'd met a girl named Rose.

He hadn't planned for a girl to enter his life. He had too many other problems to even think about dealing with another circumstance for a while yet, but here came a girl, with the biggest brown eyes he had ever seen in his life, she just swept him off his feet. Her family lived on the road leading to the rural area where he did some of his part-time farm work and he went by her house most days. She worked in a cotton mill near Thomasville, a town just a few miles further down the road, so he had learned to time his passing with the days he knew she would be home.

"Howdy," he would say politely when he'd catch a glimpse of her in the yard or out back hanging clothes on the line. He knew she had lots of brothers and sisters and she appeared to be maybe the oldest. At least the oldest girl.   The siblings would stop and stare at him whenever he tried to talk to Rose.   He wished they would go away so he could talk to Rose more, maybe they could even sit down in the swing and talk for a spell and he could get to know her better.

"I see you aren't at the cotton mill today. I expect the work is slow?"

"Yes it is.   Some weeks I get only two days.   They used to work us at least six days and that was usually for ten hours.   Now I work only two and the hours are short besides."

"I know how hard it is.   I'm glad you have your family."

"Yes, I have my family.   It's hard on them too. My brother is looking, but he can't find work.   My papa isn't working right now either, and the money I was bringing in was all they had." Rose said sadly.

"Would you like to go to the movin' pictures this Saturday night?" Steven asked her, changing the subject abruptly.

The small theatre in Thomasville showed only silent films of the period, and they still employed a piano player.   The two found they both liked these old reels and it was just another of many things they found they had in common.   Her parents demanded that in order to take their daughter to the picture show, he had to take her

96

older brother along as chaperone. It was hard to come up with enough money to pay for three tickets, but Steven was in love and no sacrifice was too great.

Money wasn't the only problem this threesome posed. Rose's brother couldn't read so that meant having to tell him what all the sub-titles said. It became tiresome and took away from the pleasure of the evening. Fortunately, the brother soon found his own pals who frequented the movie theatre and he began sitting with them.

The courtship between the two continued on for several months, mostly with them just taking long walks or an occasional picnic when one of the farmer's gave Steven a big juicy melon. Steven learned that Rose had worked since she was only thirteen, being taken out of school to go into the cotton mill. It had broken her heart to leave school and Steven could empathize with her, knowing how much he had wanted to continue with his own education. He felt guilty, knowing Rose had been denied half the education he had.

"But I read as much as I can," Rose related bravely. " Mrs. Bailey at the library knows the kind of books I need to help educate myself. I've read everyone she has loaned me, and she says I'm doing fine."

Steven felt so proud of her, he wished he could make a better life for her. He knew that not only did she work and turn her money over to her papa, but she carried most of the weight of the housework too. He wasn't sure what ailed her mother, but he had seen many women worn out from too many babies, too closely spaced, and suspected that might be her problem. The father apparently lacked ambition, but Steven's manners did not allow him to point this out to Rose. He felt she knew.

Steven knew that he wanted to marry Rose and he was pretty sure she felt the same for him. But before bringing up the subject to her, he wanted to be sure he could provide a home for them. He went back to see Mrs. Stone at the old boarding house where he and Randolph had first lived. It was even more run down than he remembered.

"Mornin' Mrs. Stone. Do you remember me?" he asked

when he arrived.

"I sure do. How are you, Steven, and how is Randolph. I've really missed you boys," she answered happily.

They exchanged pleasantries for several minutes and then Steven got right down to business.

"You got any boarders now, Mrs. Stone?" he asked quietly, not wishing to offend the woman.

"No, they's no work to be had. Folks can't afford to pay and I can't keep 'em for nothin'." The first part of the reply was what he was hoping to hear, but not the latter.

"I've met a girl. Her name is Rose. I'm…..that is we……will most likely be getting married soon. I haven't asked her yet, but I'm pretty sure she'll say 'yes.' But before I ask her I want to be sure I have someplace for us to live."

And then, Steven laid out his plan. The boarding house was in a terrible state. The back porch was virtually falling apart, the roof needed work, the windows……..Steven pointed out some of the things he wanted to especially mention that were jobs requiring a man's strength. And he was just the man who could do the job.

"Steven, I can't pay you." Mrs. Stone reminded him.

"I know.   And I can't afford to pay you.   But couldn't we make a trade? Times are going to get better, and when they do you'll be wanting to rent out your rooms. We need to get ready for that day. Rose and me, we can help."   Steven tried his most winning smile on her and whether it was the smile, the reasoning, or just loneliness, Mrs. Stone agreed to allow Steven and Rose to have her biggest room, in exchange for the work they would do.

"And if you still get some of those good country vegetables or canned goods, would you share with an old lady?" she asked.

"You know I will," he replied.   And Mrs. Stone did know. She knew Steven to be a hard working, honest boy ……. now grown to manhood……. who was always there to help another.   He had a good heart.

CHAPTER 21

And so the day arrived when Steven and Rose would be wed. Rose's mother wept when she was told the news, and gave Rose a heartfelt hug and wished her well. She wanted better things for her Rose than working in a cotton mill. Rose was a smart girl and her mother knew she could do better. "Steven is a real good boy," her mother told her. "I have faith he will take good care of you."

Rose's mother had only one valued possession and that was a clock her own parents had given her on her wedding day. She wanted Rose to have it. It made Rose cry to accept it, knowing what it meant to her mother but after much persuasion, had taken it with her. Rose knew she would treasure it always, and her mother knew this too.

Steven wrote to Harold, Susan, Will and Rodney to invite them to the small wedding. Randolph was there to stand up with them and while Susan nor Will could make the trip, they did respond with heartfelt congratulations and much appreciated wedding gifts. Will and Miss Alvira, or Allie as he called her now, sent a beautiful hand made quilt and Susan had a set of dishes shipped all the way from Philadelphia. There was no reply from Harold or Rodney. No one from Rose's family choose to join them.

The couple moved into their new quarters at Mrs. Stone's boarding house. There had been an ulterior motive to Steven seeking out a place in High Point. Of course since he already had ties with Mrs. Stone it was a logical choice, but he also wanted to move Rose as far as he could away from her family. He had noted she worked very hard every day, but she had sisters nearly full grown who could take over the work load. They spent their days putting cheap polish on their nails, rolling their hair and plucking their eyebrows. He knew if he and Rose settled close by, her papa would still expect Rose to come every day and continue with her 'chores.' Steven wanted Rose to be near enough for frequent visits, but not close enough to be expected to do the work. He intended to see that some of the others took that burden off his Rose's shoulders.

The newlyweds were very happy in their new life and Rose helped Mrs. Stone to do both her 'fall and spring cleaning.' As far as Mrs. Stone was concerned, Rose was a jewel and she loved having her around.

"Rose, I surely do need to do some mending on these sheets," Mrs. Stone told her one day. "When the house was full, it took a lot of sheets for all the beds but they are thin and worn. I believe we can turn them. If we split them in half, then sew the outside edges together, they look to still be alright, it will give us a few more years of wear." As the two ladies cut and stitched, they enjoyed a cup of tea and lots of women talk. Rose came to love the old lady and was glad Steven had brought her here. When they had finished all their stitching, Mrs. Stone insisted Rose keep the best set of sheets for herself.

"You'll need these someday when you and Stevie have a place of your own," she told her.

Rose tucked the sheets away with her few other small housekeeping possessions, those things one might call a 'hope chest' and it made Mrs. Stone happy to see that Rose appreciated even the most meager of gifts. She wished she had more to share. Mrs. Stone felt taking in this young couple was the best decision she had ever made. Steven still found just enough work to keep 'a few coins in his pocket' as he liked to say, and continued to bring home fresh vegetables too. As always in the summer time there is more than one can eat, all ripening at once, and so Mrs. Stone brought out the jars from her cellar and with Rose's help, they 'put by' some canned goods for winter. Rose had never tried her hand at preserving before but Mrs. Stone was patient and showed the young bride just how to put away canned tomatoes, corn and green beans.

Rose's jobs were at first the easier tasks, such as washing all the jars and the zinc lids. But further into the canning and preserving chores, she began to work with the rubber rings, learning how to inspect against small nicks and cracks, and how to run the knife around the bottom of the zinc lid after the jar was filled with vegetables for canning, pressing it snuggly against the rubber ring for a

100

good, clean seal. It was hard work, but a thrilling experience as she saw the beautiful jars of canned goods lined up in the cellar, awaiting the day they would be prepared for the table and served with pride. And in the meantime Steven had plenty of time to work on the boarding house.

"The boards on the porch have rotted so badly, I'll need to throw some of them away," he told Mrs. Stone.

"We'll just use them in the wood stove then, Stevie. But can you do anything to restore the porch?"

"Oh, yes'm. But the porch may have to be shortened a bit. I'll use all the good boards and build it back, good as new, but just not quite as big," he answered. She had watched as the old porch had slowly sagged and then dropped away from the main frame. A porch, any porch of any size, was good news to her.

And so the work and their time spent with Mrs. Stone continued. It could have been a story book marriage with all things blissful, but the time wasn't right. The country was still in a depression and that recovery they were all looking for hadn't happened. It might not happen for several years.

The winter months were here now and Steven's farm hand jobs had run out. Rose tried to find work, but the cotton mills were still laying off, not hiring. Steven wrote to his old friend, Joe, back in Virginia. He had an idea in mind. It wasn't long until Steven had his answer. Steven would have to write to Aunt Nora and ask her for it personally, but yes, the old cabin on the Carterson farm property was empty. It didn't have running water, but Steven knew about the good spring close by, and there was even a privy out back. It was two rooms, a bedroom and a kitchen, but it was better than having nothing. It was one of the hardest things he had tried to do, but Steven sat down and wrote Aunt Nora the necessary letter.

Dear Steven, her response began, *We were surprised to hear from you after all this time, but thought we would be hearing eventually.* Did she mean I would come crawling back? He smarted at her possible insinuation, but continued reading. *I am glad you are well. Frances and I are just fine. The little house is empty as you thought, and you and your bride, Rose, can use it if you are wanting to come back here. There is a good spring. We don't do much farming since George passed away, but I would expect you to help some with the work that does need doing in exchange for rent. Our horses and farm equipment are still here, and we will discuss your specific duties after you arrive. Aunt Nora and Frances.*

Steven could almost feel the coldness in her words and could well imagine the work load he would have to take on 'in exchange for rent' as she put it. But he'd have some time for farming a bit on his own, and knew he could borrow the horses and equipment for his own use whenever Aunt Nora didn't demand them. It wasn't going to be a rosy future back on the Carterson farm, but he and Rose wouldn't go hungry.

"I'm sorry, Rose, I hoped to be a good husband to you, but the whole country is out of work right now." Steven said humbly.

"Do you think I don't know that?" she answered and kissed his cheek.

"I don't know if you'll like Virginia. As for me, it's not the place itself that troubles me. It just holds lots of bad memories."

"Then I guess we got to make some good memories, don't we?" she answered confidently. She loved Steven and being with him was all that mattered. She hid her fears from him, knowing he had enough on his mind and knowing he was doing his best to take care of her. She knew nothing about farm life. She knew from reading her books that farmer's grew their own chickens and wrung their necks for Sunday dinner. She was a town girl. She knew only that chickens come from the market, bare skin showing and nothing inside. What in the world would she do? But she kept this and her other fears to herself.

The two shared their plans with Mrs. Stone and while she would be sorry to see them go she understood that something must be done. The couple had no money for even the basic necessities. Steven would sell a few meager possessions to raise money for the fare to Virginia. Rose would stay on with Mrs. Stone until he could raise a crop and sell it. It might take eight or nine months for him to

102

get the money together, but he would send for Rose as soon as he could.

"I will grieve for you everyday until I know I'm coming too," Rose told him, crying.

"And I promise to work hard to get the money together just as soon as I can." Steven vowed.

Before the day arrived for his planned departure, two letters arrived in the mail. Steven had written to his siblings to let them know of his plan, and here was an envelope from Will with a small amount of money inside. A second letter from Susan contained a bit more money......enough money all together with what Steven had already put aside for two train tickets to Abingdon. They would be going together, and with their possessions being so few they could even carry their precious wedding gifts with them.

Before Rose was to leave, she paid one last visit to her mother. It was very upsetting to her mother to know she would not see her daughter often, or if ever again. It was a long way to the mountains of Virginia. But even as she said goodbye, Rose's mother was happy for her daughter. She saw how Steven had provided a home for Rose, it was a small place, but clean and neat and she was proud. She wished Rose all the best and hugged her tight. Rose's mother couldn't read or write, but some of her sisters could. Rose promised her mother she would send letters often, and she should get one of the other girls to read it to her. And they could put down her mother's words and write back to Rose. Rose's sisters seemed to resent her leaving and pouted as she left. They didn't promise anything.

Steven and Rose said goodbye to Randolph and headed for the farm lands of Virginia. They arrived at the train depot in Abingdon and were met by cousin Frances. Steven couldn't help but wonder if his entire life was going to be centered around this one little depot in Abingdon. Every important moment in his life seemed to happen here.

"This Rose?" Frances asked in her usual and abrupt manner.

"This is my wife, Rose. Rose, I would like to introduce you to my cousin Frances." Steven said in his most social voice.

"I'm so pleased to meet you," Frances replied. She noted

103

from Steve's exaggerated tone, he was most likely pointing out her own lack of manners. Sounded like something Dottie would do.

Frances drove the young couple to their home, a dilapidated two room shack by most standards. Rose was appalled but would never let Steven know. She appeared undaunted by it's condition and simply set to work making it a home. She didn't know if there were lice or vermin, or both. But this was her home now and if they were current inhabitants, they would have to leave. She was taking over!

Within hours the bare floors were scrubbed and cob webs removed from the corners and overhead. There was an oil lamp which thankfully still worked and she trimmed the wick and washed the sooty globe. Steven had hauled in lots of water for her, and had started a fire in the cook stove. At first the smoke billowed out into the room, but now it was drawing nicely. Rose unpacked her precious dishes and placed them on a crude shelf in the kitchen. She took out her mother's clock and put it in a place of honor in the small room.

Aunt Nora had provided them with some dried beans and side meat. The meat smelled a little rancid, but then Steven would not have expected anything else. The beans had been cooking as they worked, and they sat down to enjoy them. A bed frame with a thin, well stained cotton mattress was all that occupied the bedroom Rose spread her patched sheets brought from Mrs. Stone's place in North Carolina over the mattress and topped it with the beautiful wedding quilt. They were home. When it rained they found the roof leaked, when the cold winds blew they found the cracks in the siding and around the windows, but still they were home.

And home it would become for the three of them, for by the end of the first year in the little house, a son was born.

"He's so beautiful," Steven cooed. "And you're sure about the name?"

"Yes," Rose replied. "He'll be called Randolph." As they had already discussed, the name they would use would be Randy. That way they could always distinguish between the two Randolphs and avoid any confusion.

104

Steven immediately wrote to his siblings. The first letter went to Randolph for whom the baby was named and then a letter went off to Susan. He hesitated over writing to Harold. No word had come despite his many attempts and he felt a letter was in vain. And so the last letter he sent was to Rodney. There had been no reply to his previous correspondence, he wasn't even sure if Rodney received his letters. But he had placed a return address on them, and he only knew the letters had not come back to him.

After posting the letters, Steven left Rose alone long enough to ride over to Miss Alvira's farm to see Will. Even though Will was a grown man now and had the urge to strike out on his own, he felt he owed Miss Alvira too much to leave her. She was growing old, and he knew their roles had changed, it was now his place to care for her.

Steven rode one of the plow horses since that was the only transportation available to him. Steven and Will were as close as ever since Steven had returned to Virginia and they visited often. Will had awaited the birth nearly as anxiously as Steven himself.

Word had already spread about the good news and Will was in fact on his way to Steven's house. They recognized one another and Will quickly pulled Alvira's automobile to the side of the road.

"I've come to see the new baby. I hear you're gonna call him Randy." Will said after he and Steven disembarked from their very different modes of transportation.

"Yeah. And he's a Williams through and through. Got a head of hair, just like mine only maybe not quite as unruly. His momma will see to that. You're coming to the house to see him aren't you?" Steven asked.

And that's just what he did, but not only to see the new baby boy but also to say goodbye. He had withheld his plans until after the baby came.

*****

"But why are you going into the navy, Will? You've never even seen the ocean," Steven asked incredulously.

"It's a dream I've had for a long, long time." Will answered

105

simply. "I didn't think I could ever do this, but Allie, Alvira, has decided to leave the farm. She wants to move in closer to town with her niece. She's not well, and she knows it. She told me I could stay on at the farm for as long as I wanted to call it home, but I told her about my dreams of the navy. She understands."

"I can't believe we're going to be separated again." Steven said slowly.

"I know. But you have Rose and the baby now. And I'll be coming home on leave. I'm nineteen now, 'most twenty. If I'm ever going, it's got to be now."

Will was to leave for training camp within the next two weeks. He didn't seem to feel any homesickness over his decision, only an impatience for his new journey to begin.

Will saw to getting his sweet Allie moved into town, and helped the new renters move into the house he had known as home for nearly all of his life. He saved his last day for Steven, Rose and the baby.

The four of them had a wonderful day together, Will holding and rocking his little nephew to sleep. Rose had not regained her full strength so Steven helped cook up a pot of October beans with some fried potatoes, but they had to call on Rose to help with the cornbread. Steven just didn't have the hang of it, and Rose's cornbread was mouth-watering good. And then, Will bade them goodbye, but with the promise to keep in touch.

He would be leaving from the train depot in Abingdon, but insisted that Steven not try to make the trip, his place was at home taking care of Rose. Steven was heartbroken to see Will go but felt he could handle the goodbye better this way. Another farewell at the train depot might have been more than his emotions could manage.

CHAPTER 22

A few days later, the first letter from Rodney arrived. In the same mail was a beautiful card from Susan and many, many warm clothes for the baby. Steven put Rodney's letter aside for a few minutes while he and Rose marveled over all the precious little clothes. They held each outfit in front of Randy as though he could actually see what his Aunt Susan had sent him. The young couple were without many possessions of their own, and it hurt to deny their baby even the most fundamental items. But the ever-giving, sweet Susan had thought of everything. God bless her.

While Rose looked at all the little clothes again, then folded them carefully and placed them on the bed to look at a while longer, Steven went into the kitchen to read Rodney's letter.

As the letter began he was very withdrawn and stolid, but as he kept writing, the hopelessness began to creep into his message. He appeared to have some memory of his past, but didn't know if it was really a memory or just what he wanted to believe. He did not recall either parent, but said he thought he might recall Will. *Did I ever call him Willy when I was young?* he asked. But it was his words, *'I seem to recall a lady hugged me once, and cried,'* that gave Steven cause for unrest. He spoke of being hugged in the past tense, as if it had not happened again except for his vague memory. Could that be possible?

"Rose, when I needed him most, Randolph sent me a way out. I think I owe it to Rodney to pass along the favor." Steven said, mulling over the letter. "I can't put my finger on it. He doesn't accuse. But something is wrong."

Rose, too, read the letter and sensed a problem. It was not a specific line but the entire letter. It was as though there were an undercurrent. Something they couldn't see but could only feel.

"Do what you feel you must, Steven. I will stand behind your decision." Rose answered. And he knew she meant it with all her heart.

107

Several more letters were exchanged over the next three months until Steven got a clear picture of what life must have been like at the Miners. Rodney needed his brother, even more than Steven had needed help those years ago. Following his older brother's example, Steven was able to sell enough eggs and other produce at the market to get together the money to send Rodney a bus ticket. It wasn't a problem of distance, Damascus was not that far, but it wouldn't pay to pull into the Miner's driveway in Aunt Nora's old car and try to take Rodney away. Dr. Miner was still Rodney's legal guardian, so therefore, they would keep their plans and later Rodney's whereabouts a secret, at least until they could figure out what to do. The ticket Steven sent was one with no specific date, one Rodney could use any time he could get away and come to be with him, Rose and the baby.

I will come soon, Rodney had written, *I am having a fever just now and am not able to travel. As soon as I am strong enough I will come. I cannot tell anyone here about my plans to leave.*

Steven answered that his bed was ready, not prying any deeper into what was obviously a very troubled young man. He only hoped he could help Rodney to heal the wounds, whatever they were. There was actually very little space in the house for the family of three and he knew it would be hard to manage another person in their small quarters, but Steven would not say that. Aunt Nora had loaned him a pallet for the floor. He hadn't directly lied to Aunt Nora but had implied it was for some of Rose's relatives who might be visiting from Carolina. They would unroll it in the kitchen each night. The pallet was where Rodney would bed down. Steven suspected it might even have been his own pallet from the loft, but had the good grace to just thank Aunt Nora for her kindness. No use bringing up old hurts, was there?

With one more exchange of letters between the two, a tentative date was set. Steven drove to Abingdon. He was driving Aunt Nora's old car. Since there had been many errands he needed to take care of for her, she had decided his riding horseback was too slow and had instructed Frances to teach him how to operate the stick shift. He proudly drove into the parking lot of the Greyhound bus station. He pulled into a parking space and went inside to wait. He looked around and realized the place had not changed all that much. It had looked bigger and more ominous the night he had waited here when he ran away from the farm, but knew that was only his own perception at the time. The place still held a lot of bad memories but Steven wouldn't allow himself to think about them. He was here for Rodney now, and that's all that mattered.

At last the bus pulled into the station. It came in at much too fast a speed and the driver fairly skidded the bus into its regular parking space. The driver leaped from the bus and ran inside, excited and shouting.

"We got a doctor around here? I need a doctor. Real quick," the bus driver yelled. He was flushed and extremely upset about something.

"Who's sick?" asked Steven, who happened to be the person closest to the arriving bus.

"You a doc?"

"No," Steven answered. There was a terrible sinking in the pit of his stomach. "But my brother is on that bus."

"Got a boy on there, all right. Think he dead," the driver cried out. No doubt his training had not covered what to do in an emergency. Nor did it cover tact.

Steven's blood ran cold. He quickly boarded the bus. The passengers had all kept their seats, apparently ordered to do so by the driver. They appeared extremely upset, some were crying quietly, not knowing what else to do.

"Where?" was all he said. The passengers pointed to a young man sitting about half way back, his head laying against the window. His eyes were open and glazed over. His mouth hung open just a bit and there were traces of blood on his lips and around his ears.

Steven hadn't seen Rodney for quite a while, but there was no denying those Williams looks. He grabbed Rodney and held him close. He stroked his cheek and hair..

"Rodney?" he queried, sobbing loudly and making no attempt to hide his grief. His brother was only seventeen years old. You weren't supposed to be dead when you were seventeen. "Rodney?"

109

he begged again.

There was no answer. Steven knew from the feel of him that Rodney was gone. He continued to hold him and rock his brother's unresponsive body back and forth as he crooned an old lullaby he remembered his mother singing to them. The passengers left the bus, unnoticed. The bus depot manager tried to get Steven to leave, but Steven shouted for him to go away. The manager left also. Finally a doctor did arrive and pried Steven's arms from around the body of his dead brother.

"What happened? He was coming to stay with me," Steven cried. He knew he was out of control, but didn't care. This was his baby brother. He was supposed to look after him.

"I don't know, but just looking I would guess he had pneumonia. The blood would indicate maybe his lungs have burst. Without further examination, I just don't know," the doctor told him as gently as he could.

Steven and Rose bought a space in the little cemetery at the Green Springs Baptist Church near their home and where they attended regularly. Susan came to be with them and once again Steven drove Aunt Nora's old car, this time to the train station, to meet her. Rose and Susan became instant friends, partly because they were so alike, and perhaps partly because they shared the love of the same persons. Steven slept on the pallet meant for Rodney and allowed Susan to share the regular bed with Rose. It was pleasant with overtones of sadness as Susan played with her nephew for the first time, but deeply melancholy because they had lost Rodney before they even had a true chance to find him again. Will had already left for boot camp. Randolph was not at his last known boarding house, he had moved elsewhere temporarily to seek work and the message did not reach him in time for the funeral, and once again there was no reply from Harold. After discussion with Rose and Susan, it was decided not to inform the Miner family. They would learn of it eventually.

As they lowered Rodney's casket, Steven said goodbye to one more of his own. The openness of the grave gave a scent of the earth and it filled Steven's nostrils. For a moment he was trans-

110

ported in his mind to another place, another time. He was seven years old again and he was hiding under a porch. Rose squeezed his hand as if she knew his thoughts.

They returned to the house and Susan held little Randy as if she could never let go. She rocked him and crooned softly until he fell asleep.

"I helped my mother with Will and Rodney, and I think it must be the most wonderful thing on earth to have a little one of your very own," she said wistfully.

"But you still have plenty of time for that, Susan. There's no reason for you to think you won't have a baby of your own some-day," Rose protested.

"I don't think so. I don't feel I will ever marry. I guess I'm going to be the spinster, the 'old maid,'" she said.

"Why in the world would say such a thing? You are a lovely young woman. Any man would be proud to make you his wife." Rose didn't understand why Susan sounded so sad.

"I don't even know how to flirt," she said, trying to laugh. "I watch the other nurses, and they can attract a man by just batting their eyelashes. I wouldn't even know how to do that." She spoke as if in a jolly way, but Rose suspected it was truly how she felt.

"Nonsense, you are very attractive and you don't have to 'bat' your eyelashes at anyone."

"If I had a husband, if there was someone in my life, I would be so afraid of losing him. Just like Momma lost our Papa. It has been so hard to give up those we love, I could never give up my husband like Momma had to do. If I had a husband, I would hold on to him for dear life. I could never let him go." Susan said this so vehemently it almost scared Rose.

"Dear, you mustn't fear what happened to your parents would happen to you too," was all Rose could think to say.

Susan stayed for a few days only, and soon it was time she return to her nursing job in Philadelphia. Steven drove her into town and said goodbye to her at the depot. He watched sadly as the train carried her away once more. And then he stopped by the funeral home to pay what he could on Rodney's expenses. The doctor he

111

had seen at the bus station was just leaving.

"I've filled out the final paperwork on your brother's death certificate. I stopped by to leave a copy for their files," he told Steven. He paused as if he wanted to say more.

"Then it was pneumonia, far as you know?" asked Steven.

"Yes, but well I don't know what good it does to tell you now, but there were signs of abuse to that boy. And not just recent, but many old scars. Even a few broken bones that hadn't healed properly. I'm sorry, son, but I believe your brother was treated very poorly." The doctor shook his head and walked away. Didn't need to tell too much, he thought, the horror he expected had happened to that poor boy didn't need to be spoken. It was too late to help, but maybe the brother would know what to do if there were others in harm's way.

The doctor's comments would add heavily to the grief Steven would bear, and he would forever blame himself for not seeking out his brother sooner and rescuing him from this awful fate.

CHAPTER 23

Being the head of a household now, Steven felt the need to work harder and provide a more suitable home for he and his family. The years spent in Aunt Nora's cabin had not improved his financial standing very much as he had to share any crop money with her, that's the way it worked when you lived on someone else's place. The hail had ruined his tobacco crop one year, nearly wiping them out. Steven wanted more for his family.

He'd heard about a small farm for sale. The old gentleman who owned it had passed away, and his son-in-law already had more farmland then he could handle so had persuaded his wife to put the home place on the market. Steven and Rose drove to Meadowview and to the farm site. The house itself was not in much better shape than the one they would be leaving on Aunt Nora's farm. It had a sagging roof and ill fitting windows. The chimney was in obvious need of repair, but it did have four rooms as opposed to only two. That was a big step forward and Rose was very excited at the prospect of having a separate room she could call the parlor, and a spare room for the baby. Steven watched her eyes light up as she walked about, room to room, envisioning the curtains she would make, where she would put each piece of furniture, when they got some furniture that is.

They walked around the yard and the garden space. There were several acres of fertile land and there was a barn and some outbuildings. The barn needed a new roof, but Steven thought he could repair it with a few pieces of tin.

"It's too good to be true," Rose spoke finally. "I know it needs a lot of work right now, but................."

"That's what I'm thinking, too. It would be a good home for us, we can fix it up, make it better. I'm just afraid it is way over our heads, even for this small place. I'm worried about going to the bank and even asking for a loan." Steven spoke in a soft voice, as if he didn't want to be overheard and cast a hex on the possibility.

"But let's ask anyway," Rose pleaded.

"I'll do that. They can always say no, but if I don't at least try we'll always wonder, won't we?"

First thing Monday morning, Steven put on his best suit. It was a little shiny and didn't fit as good as it once did, but off he went to the People's National Bank on the corner of Wall and West Main Street in Abingdon. The loan officer was polite, but it was evident he wasn't going to be able to help. At least not with a loan, but his help proved to be invaluable in other ways.

"I can't in good conscience loan you this much money on a farm," he said. At Steven's crestfallen expression he continued on, "We have had so many foreclosures in the last few years, we just can't take a chance on another farm right now. But if you don't mind my interference, I do have some suggestions."

"By all means," Steven said, his ears ready for some good news.

"On checking your name in our files, I do find that you have an amount on deposit in a trust fund. Are you aware of that?"

"No," Steven fairly whispered his answer. Could this be true? But how?

"When your father's estate was settled, I believe it was the sale of a general store, maybe two, there was an amount of money put in the bank in trust. The two gentlemen, I believe them to be your uncles, Mason and Basil White, are the custodians. They can withdraw the interest earned each year, but that is all. The majority of your principal, and that of your siblings, is intact."

His mother had told them the money was being put aside for them, but his uncles had told it differently. They said the money was gone, lost on bad investments. Even in the midst of this joyful news, Steven did momentarily take note that the loan officer had said 'your principal' is still intact. He was sure his uncles had been withdrawing the interest all along, something the law would allow them to do so there was no wrong doing, legally that is. But Steven was so happy to find there was money to be had, he didn't waste his time with anger.

"I thought the money was gone." Steven said.

114

"Some of it is. Lost with the stock market crash. But the largest part was in low-yield investments and is secure."

"How much? All I care about is, will there be enough for a suitable down payment?" Steven asked.

"Yes, I'm sure it will be. The money is in the name of six of the children, I believe there were five boys and a daughter. The money is to be divided equally and disbursed when you reach the age of eighteen. But I can see you fulfill that requirement. If any of the six of you should be deceased prior to age eighteen, the funds due that sibling will be disbursed equally among the remaining."

"We had no way of knowing the money was still available to us. We were led to believe it was gone a very long time ago."

"Then that would explain why none of you came forward to make a claim."

"One of my brothers has died. Rodney. He was only seventeen."

"I'm sorry to hear that. If you have a copy of his death certificate, I will place it on file with the bank's records. You might want to mention this inheritance to your other siblings. The bank had no idea you did not know about the money. Our only dealings have been with Misters Mason and Basil White. We simply assumed you were leaving the money for an investment when times are better."

"I'll take care of the details. And I'm sure my brothers and sister will be just as shocked as I," Steven told him.

"And now, for my other suggestion. You say the farm you wish to purchase is located near Meadowview. There is a small bank in Meadowview and I feel that is where you should go. We are so limited here with times being as they are, and we feel we must service the local folks first. It might be easier to arrange a loan through your Meadowview bank. And now you'll have a good down payment, besides."

Steven left the bank with wings beneath his feet. He had loved Papa so much, Papa had always taken care of them. And now, even years after his death, Papa was still taking care of them.

Steven did visit that bank in Meadowview and with an

adequate down payment, the bank approved his loan. He also took a copy of Rodney's death certificate to the Abingdon bank as requested. He hoped his siblings would withdraw their money and place it in another account. He didn't want the uncles drawing out the interest from Papa's money ever again.

By the time the now three-year-old Randy was toddling around, the little family was securely moved to their own modest farm near a town called Meadowview. Several good pieces of farm equipment had been left for the new owner, the son-in-law taking the better pieces, but Steven wasn't complaining. He was good at fixin' things up and this was not a worry to him. A good team of horses was a worry, but he had been so fortunate so far, he felt surely the Good Lord and his Papa were watching after him and everything was going to be all right.

Steven received a check for his portion of the money that would have gone to Rodney. He felt guilty about receiving these funds and had difficulty accepting it. He put the check up and didn't cash it. At Rose's urging, he finally agreed to spend the money on a pair of draft horses. He wanted to feel that somehow Rodney knew, and would approve. Steven searched for a way to say 'thank you' to Rodney. He named the horses Penny and Sam after the two pet ducks Rodney had loved as a child but had left behind in Greeneville, Tennessee so many years ago.

"We will be happy here," Rose declared. Somehow she knew she had finally arrived at the home she and Steven had talked about when they first met. Their sparse furnishings were lost in the bigger house, but Rose had a way of making it look cozy. She collected colorful feed sacks and set about making curtains for the kitchen and bedroom windows. The parlor would have to wait until the sale of tobacco in the fall. Those needed to be 'store bought' curtains. And maybe they could get a nice settee.

Rose sat down and wrote her mother a letter. She wanted to give her mother her new address even though she had received almost no word from home since she had moved to Virginia. Just a short note at first, and then one when Randy was born. But she wrote glowingly about the new farm, just as if they wrote every month.

116

She tried to show her happiness and the promise of the future. She knew her mother would be happy for her.

"Will has written and said he'll be on leave next month. His ship is in port at Newport News and he'll have some time off." Steven told her.

"Then you must have him come and stay with us. We can set up a cot in Randy's room, if Will won't mind sharing." Rose replied.

"If you're sure it won't be too hard on you. I'd love to see him again. I've missed him very much," Steven told her.

"I know he has missed you just as much. I think one of the reasons he decided to make a career in the Navy was he didn't have family to come back to." Rose answered. "Let's see if we can make him feel this is his home, too." She knew that his custodian, Miss Alvira, had died last year leaving Will without any close connections. She had left most of her farm to Will, the other half going to her niece, and Will had made arrangements for a long term lease on his half. He had no plans to return permanently anytime soon. Rose felt confident they could make Will feel their home was his own, but that was not the only brother who would do so.

"Rose, I've got a message here from Randolph," he told her a few days later, just coming in from the mail box at the end of the lane.

CHAPTER 24

"It must be bad news," Rose said. She noted the expression on Steven's face as he held the letter from Randolph and knew it could not be good.

"He's sick. He wants to come here for awhile. He says he might have to go to a hospital, but he wants to come see us first," Steven went on.

"Of course, that's exactly what he must do. I would love to see him again. I've missed his sense of humor. Write back to him at once."

Randolph arrived just before Will's leave was up. Randolph's frail body was in contrast to Will's healthy, robust look. Not wanting to take away from the joy, Steven asked no questions. Borrowing a bed frame from a neighboring farmer, Steven set up a bed for the two brothers, moving Randy in with him and Rose for awhile. The brothers had a glorious reunion and sent a wire for Susan to join them. They took the cot originally intended for Will, and moved that into the sparsely furnished parlor for Susan. She couldn't pass up the opportunity to see her brothers again, and wired back her arrival time.

She would arrive at the same old train depot in Abingdon. At least this is a happy occurrence, Steven thought. For a while he had believed the depot to be jinxed, he had so many unhappy memories centering around it.

The three brothers took their places in Aunt Nora's old car for the trip to fetch Susan. Steven drove with Will in the front seat beside him, Randolph stretching his long frame out in the back. The old car was kept at Steven's on a permanent basis now. Since Frances had developed cataracts she had been afraid to drive so they had to rely on Steven to take them to the doctor or into town for supplies. Aunt Nora had installed one of those 'new fangled telephones' and had no qualms about ringing up Central and telling her to get Steven on the line. This was both a good and a bad thing. At least Steven

119

did have transportation now, but had to be ready to assist his aunt whenever he was needed. But it was a situation he could live with.

Waiting at the station, they at last saw the puffs of smoke which announced the imminent arrival of the train. This one had those fancy Pullman cars and the men folk knew that's where their sister would be. They saw the piles of luggage before they saw her.

"That's Susan's luggage," Steven told them.

"How do you know?"

"For one, I've seen it before but even if I hadn't, I'd still know it was hers. How many women take two dozen dresses for a weekend visit?" Steven was laughing as it said it. He knew half the contents of all those boxes and bags were going to be gifts for Randy, with lots thrown in for himself and Rose. Probably presents for Will and Randolph, too.

Just as he spoke, Susan came off the train wearing an exquisite hat and cape. She was the classiest lady around, and her brothers were so proud of her. They swooped her up and spun her around, one by one hugging her and telling her how great she looked. It was the first time in a long while that the four siblings had been together. It was to be one of their happiest times.

"Tell me all about navy life," Susan demanded of Will, once they had gotten into the vehicle. That had been a challenge in itself, with so much luggage and very little space. Besides tying several boxes on the back, Randolph ended up holding one of the cases on his lap.

"It's really great. You know I've never been anywhere except this little corner of Virginia and a few miles across the Tennessee line. Now I've got the whole world to see."

"And you, Randolph. Steven wrote you haven't been well, but you look much better than I expected. You have so much color in your cheeks." Susan told him.

"That's because Steven keeps me in the field all day. I get plenty of sun." Randolph laughed as he spoke.

"Just following doctor's orders." Steven told him. "Lots of sunshine and fresh air." The group was in high spirits and the questions flew, each bringing the other up to date on their separate lives.

120

Over the sound of the many happy voices, there was a loud bang followed by a hissing and a thumping sound.

"Drat. A flat tire," moaned Steven.

"I don't mind the flat so much, but you know we gotta unload all Susan's junk to get to the repair kit and the pump," Randolph said, pretending to be greatly distressed.

"Watch what you are calling junk, brother dear." Susan replied, hitting him on the back of his head, but ever so lightly.

Pulling to the side of the road, all of them stepped out of the automobile and began piling Susan's many cases on the ground. At last they could get to the jack and made quick work of getting the tire off. After deflating it completely, they pulled the tube from inside the tire.

"You don't have a spare, I guess?" asked Will.

"I'm lucky to have four tires, you don't really think we can afford five?" Steven asked, but he was laughing as he said it.

"Where's the tube repair kit?" Randolph asked.

Steven already had it out and the three men went about patching the inner tube. After giving the patch time to set, they replaced it and began working with the manual air pump. They replaced the tire on the automobile and continued pumping air into the tube until they felt it was sufficiently filled. Then they released the jack and lowered the automobile back to the surface. The tire still looked a little flat so they worked at pumping more air into it. The task was far more than Randolph could handle, but with Will in excellent condition from his Navy training, the job was done. They began piling Susan's luggage back into and on back of the vehicle. It wasn't long before they pulled into the farm and saw Rose waiting.

"Come on in, you weary travelers. I've got cold lemonade for everyone," she shouted.

Rose ran to the automobile and hugged Susan warmly. Rose noted the men looked a little scruffy and dirty, and figured she knew the reason for their being late. She didn't want to put a damper on the occasion so thought she would wait until later to ask Steven about it. Little Randy had followed his mother and was waiting to be picked up. Susan was happy to comply.

"Oh my goodness. You have gotten so very, very big!" Randy ducked his head shyly and knew somehow that what was said was a good thing.

There would be no more work this day, this was a day of relaxation and sheer pleasure. Except of course the milking must be done. That's one a farmer can't postpone. And so the six of them; Rose and Randy, along with Randolph, Will and Susan, went out to the barn with Steven, none being able to tear themselves away from the others even long enough to do the chores. The next few days flew by much too quickly and all too soon they knew it must end.

*****

"Will, do you really have to go so soon?" they all asked.

"Yeah, I really do. I'm due back on ship by no later than the 17th of the month. I gotta go now to make it," he had answered. He had loved every minute of being with his family again, but he loved the navy, too. It has become his new home and he was looking forward to his new assignment in Hawaii. He had been assigned to the USS Arizona, a choice assignment for any enlisted man.

"Keep in touch with us," they all begged. And Will had dutifully promised to do just that.

They all returned home and soon, too, Susan had to leave them to return to her duties and her own apartment in Philadelphia. She had talked in glowing terms about her work and a new man she had met. She had seen him only twice, she'd explained, but somehow she just felt 'good' about him. From the radiance in her face when she spoke of him, Steven was hopeful she might find happiness with this person. It had taken Susan many years to get over the death of her mother. She felt that as her mother's caretaker there should have been something she could have done to save her. She felt it was her fault her mother had died so soon. But now she was trying to get on with her life. Susan was a beautiful person, both inside and out. Steven would pray for her happiness.

Randolph wouldn't be saying goodbye, at least not for a time. His condition was deteriorating, and Rose kept persuading him to stay just a little longer.

"Just until your strength comes back," she would add.

Randolph was happy with Steven and Rose. And he loved little Randy and rejoiced that Rose was once again pregnant. He hoped he would be around for the arrival of baby number two. Some days he really did feel stronger, other days he doubted it. But on the good days he could follow Steven into the fields and try to earn his keep, as he called it.

"You sure you goin' need this much corn?" Randolph would ask his brother.

"Yep, just keep on hoeing," would be his laughing reply.

Although there were many days Randolph could not help at all, the work he was able to perform was invaluable as Steven could not afford to hire any help right now. Some days working alone, and other days with the two of them working side by side, Steven planted and harvested his tobacco and corn. He raised a little wheat too, but mostly just for the table. He'd trade enough of the wheat to pay for having it ground into flour. The corn was mostly to feed his cows through the winter since he was trying to sell the milk for a twice monthly check from the local dairy. Tobacco was his biggest cash crop, this being a once a year sale that would pay off big things like the payment on the farm, the taxes, fire insurance, and catch him up on any doctor bills he might owe. Steven would also get a load of coal delivered to keep them warm through the winter. Tobacco selling time was a time of celebration. And the Burley crop he raised was sold just in time for Christmas......just in time for oranges, nuts, candy and the buying of big presents. The presents might not cost much apiece, but they always had to come in a big box.

And this Christmas, Steven had another special surprise for Rose. It was plans he had drawn up to start an addition onto the house. There was a lot of good timber on the land. Of course, it would take time and hard work, but if he could cut the timber and get it to the sawmill, they could use the boards to add on to the house. Rose dreamed of having a big parlor, and one more bedroom downstairs, with a second floor for two more bedrooms upstairs for company, or an expanding family.   They could do it, both Steven and Rose thought it possible.   It was a Christmas of dreams.

CHAPTER 25

"You wanted to see us?" Joe asked when he and Lelia arrived at the back door of the Merriman home. He didn't know why they had been summoned here but couldn't accept that Danny might be in trouble. Danny was a timid boy, and had never caused them worry.

Mrs. Merriman answered the door herself this time and asked them to step into the kitchen. When they were comfortably seated in the kitchen chairs she began to explain.

"Please don't be concerned," Mrs. Merriman tried to reassure them. "Danny has done nothing wrong, but I did need to let you know of some recent developments."

"Developments?" Joe wasn't sure he understood. Since Mrs. Merriman had made arrangements for Danny to study under the professor at the college, Danny had been going to the professor's house once a week on a Saturday. Joe thought everything was going well.

"I don't understand," Joe said. His voice shook, he didn't know what was going on. "I've tried to help pay for his training. I've worked and done all I know to do."

"Joe, Joe, please don't be misled. Of course you have worked hard to support Danny's training. I can't even count all the times you have mowed the lawn and refused pay, you're trimmed shrubs, pruned trees, cleared the sidewalks of ice and snow in winter. You have paid, Joe, please be assured you owe us nothing. That is not why we are here."

"I've taken a new position at another college," Professor Davis had told the Merrimans earlier. "Danny has a true gift and it has been my pleasure to work with him. But that doesn't mean my successor feel's the same." No reference was made to Danny's not being white, but the Merrimans felt that might be what he was trying to say. Obviously the replacement did not intend to carry on Danny's training and was leaving Professor Davis with the embarrassment of delivering this message.

"Danny has played at many functions in this area.   Most have been merely as background music for dinners and banquets. But he has been able to establish a name for himself.   Hopefully he will be able to find more work such as this, playing his music." Mrs. Merriman told them. She doubted her own words but needed to hear from Joe and Lelia before offering another alternative.

"Danny play some.   But most time they want to hear him play what they call 'Negro spirituals' which he happy to do. But I don't think there enough work around here to keep him busy. We been worrying about that, but he seem so happy with his lessons, we didn't want to say." Joe told her.

"Have you thought about radio?" she asked.

"Radio?"

"Yes, there is a very popular Negro minister who has his own program. He seems to have a large following. If we could write to him, get an audition for Danny, it might be a way for him to continue with his music." Mrs. Merriman continued.

"How……how we do that?" Joe asked. He was pretty sure he knew the program she was referring to, but wouldn't know how to go about getting in touch with this popular preacher.

"Professor Davis has said he will be happy to write a letter of recommendation. And I'll help you with the application if you want me to. Even if Danny is hired, I know nothing of the salary. These programs are supported through donations only, so the pay could be very low. But Danny will have an audience. Hundreds listen in each week. There is no telling where this could lead."

Joe agreed. They would miss Danny very much if he had to go away, to live in another city.   But they had come to know his music was his life. "Tell us what we needs to do first." Joe told her.

After weeks of waiting, the letter came from Reverend Archie Johnson.   Joe's hands trembled when he carried the letter to Danny to read. Danny's face showed his joy. He was going to Nashville for an audition.

Joe and Lelia never worried for a minute. They knew how great was Danny's talent and spent all their energies into getting his clothes ready for the trip. Lelia mended, washed, pressed and packed

126

his best clothes for the audition.   Joe worked extra hours at the produce warehouse to earn money for new shoes.   Now they were ready
to send their son on the road of what they hoped would be his future.

"We love you, Danny.   We know you do us proud," were
their parting words as he and his brother Joe Jr., boarded the train.
Joe Jr. would go with his younger brother as chaperone and support.
Neither of them had traveled before and Joe felt it would be best if
they traveled together.   If Danny were hired, Joe Jr. would see that
he found a good place to live.   The good Reverend Johnson would
help, they were confident of it.   And then Joe Jr. would return home
alone.   The two young men took their seat in the special car for
Negroes. They opened the window and leaned out to wave goodbye.

"Bless you son.   You write to us after you get this big radio
job," his mother called to him.   She was torn between happiness for
this chance and the sadness of saying goodbye.

"We be proud of you boys. You look after one another. Joe,
Jr. we pick you up when you get's back," their father called loudly
and boastfully.

"Danny'll show 'em what we're made of," challenged Joe
Jr.

CHAPTER 26

Steven and Randolph were in the field working, Randolph coughing a bit and leaning on his hoe, while Steven tried to pretend he didn't notice. He knew how important it was for Randolph to feel he was helping. And the doctor had said the country air was good for him. They saw Rose coming across the field, carrying water in a pail. She swung a white enamel dipper in her free hand.

"Figured you fellows could use a cold drink," she said, smiling at both of them. Her stomach was large, and her face showed the radiance some women have when they are happy with child. She rubbed her stomach and sat in the grass beside the row. The men were glad for the excuse and stopped their work to join her.

"Got a letter from Susan," she said, pulling the letter from her pocket. "She sounds real happy. Talking more about that fellow she met. Somebody nice, she says."

"Well, you gonna let me read it or tell me the whole thing?" Steven teased.

"Read it aloud, that is if nothin' in it's personal." Randolph suggested.

"I think she meant for all of us to read it," Rose assured him.

Dear family,

How I wish I was there with you. I do love my work, but sometimes it would be a good thing to be away from sick folks too. There is much pain and death here and at times it gets to me. I hope that all of you are well.

Rose, I do think about you and your condition but since you had such an easy time on your first, I feel secure this second birth will go well too. Randolph, I hope that your nagging cough is getting better. Between the good country air and Rose's cooking you should start to improve greatly. Steven, I hope both you and the farm are doing well and you are prospering. And last of all, give my sweet nephew Randy a hug from me.

129

I have some good news of my own to share. While I was with you I spoke of a wonderful man I had met. He has called me twice more and I see him whenever he is in town. He is so handsome and I think he must have money. Or at least he seems to spend a lot of it. (ha,ha) I'm not sure how old he is, he seems younger than me, but when I try to hint that maybe I am older he just says age isn't important between two people. I am a little self conscious about it, I was feeling like the old maid everyone talks about, but he makes me feel like sixteen again. I want you to meet hm.

I have to work a double shift on the critical care floor tonight so I will close for now but will try to write again soon. I love you.

Susan

"Isn't that wonderful?" squealed Rose.

"What.....that she has to work a double shift?"

"No, silly, the man she's met." Rose knew he was teasing her but she didn't mind. She was a romantic at heart and would love to see Susan happily married and perhaps even with a family of her own. There was still time.

"She says 'when he's in town.' Guess he travels then." Randolph said solemnly.

"Oh, you two always worry about everything. Be happy for her. I'd say Susan is a pretty good judge of character, wouldn't you?" Rose protested.

"I am happy for her, but you know nurses do make a good steady wage and there's no shortage of good positions available. With times hard right now, I wouldn't want to think some dandy would take advantage of her loneliness." Steven replied.

"She said he appeared to have money of his own." Rose reminded him.

"You're probably right. What's for supper?" asked Steven.

While he was concerned someone might take advantage of his sister, he agreed she had a level head and able to take care of herself. He wasn't going to waste much time pondering the possibilities.

"I guess your stomach is more important than a little love

130

between two people," Rose chided.

"Depends on which two people you're talking about," was his reply as he pulled her to her feet to plant a big kiss on her lips. Patting her behind playfully, he said "And now woman, go away so us men can get our work done."

"Thanks for the water, Rose," Randolph said gratefully. The brief rest was just what he had needed, but hated to ask.

"You're welcome. And I had better be getting back. I left Randy asleep and while I know he's alright I don't want him to wake and find me gone." She walked back across the field, once again swinging the dipper as if she were feeling very happy.

Later that evening they sat relaxing on the porch where they could pick up a soft breeze. The front porch was the only change Rose had requested to Steven's home addition plans. And they had never regretted it. As they sat resting, an old Model T stopped in front of the house. Steven recognized one of the Hyter boys, old neighbors of his when he was living at his Aunt Nora's.

"Howdy," Steven said politely, wondering why in the world this fellow was coming to call. He hadn't seen him in a long while. "Come on up on the porch and sit awhile."

"Thank ye kindly, but I need to be gettin' on. I wanted to stop by to let you know your Aunt Nora passed on. About three o'clock it was. Frances is tryin' to get hold of Dottie and she's callin' Nora's doctor in Abingdon to see what she needs to do. Guess they got to get the Coroner an' all. We got no phone ourselves, but I told Frances I'd try to get around to let the kin know. I come here first, soon as I heard." The Hyter man had continued to stand and so Steven did also.

"I really appreciate that. Can you tell me anything more? Had she been ailing the last few days?" Steven asked.

"No, don't believe so. Frances said she told her she was feeling poorly and was going to lay down on the bed for a spell. She just passed in her sleep, I reckon."

"I'll go to see Frances right away. Do you know of anything else I can do?" Steven asked.

"I knowed you had a phone. Thought maybe you might call

some of the other folks around Meadowview. I know she had kin, a brother that runs that grist mill for one. You know if he got a phone?" the Hyter man asked.

"Yes, he does. And I'll call several of Aunt Nora's kin, and I'll call Frances too to let her know I'm on the way." Steven told him.

"Then I'll be on my way. I figured I'd stop by the Smith place. They got no phone, but they is kin you know." And with that, he made his departure.

Steven went inside to telephone Frances. She was her usual abrupt self, but she did tell him more about her mother's death and the few final arrangements she had made for her. There would be a wake tomorrow night, with services and burial at the Green Springs Baptist Church the following day. Dottie and family would be arriving early tomorrow. Steven asked if he could meet them at the train station, and Frances seemed happy to have that chore taken from her shoulders.

Steven and Rose attended the wake, but Randolph felt his coughing an embarrassment and so offered to stay home and watch Randy instead. Steven could not feel a great deal of sorrow at his Aunt's death; she had lived a long and a full life. It is expected. His anger at death was when it took the young with so many years ahead. And Aunt Nora had never been a warm, loving person. But he did sympathize with Dottie. She was distraught and feeling guilty that she had moved so far away when her mother was growing older. Steven didn't know what to say to comfort her, so he just put his arms around her and patted her shoulder. Words didn't come.

Returning to the funeral service the following day, Steven's mind wandered as the pastor spoke the words of farewell. When the graveside service was over he didn't leave immediately, but walked over to where Rodney was laid. He carried with him some flowers which he had brought especially for this grave. It was a serene and peaceful place. When they had buried Rodney, Susan had remarked on the beauty of it. "Ironic," she had said, "with so much sadness here that the place could be so beautiful."

At last the tears came, but not for his Aunt Nora, the tears were for the young boy who shouldn't have been in this place.

CHAPTER 27

Rose's time was due and the doctor was summoned. She gave birth to her second child, this time a chubby little girl they named Caroline. Both Steven and Randolph paced as they waited to hear that first cry. They notified Susan as soon as possible and she came at once, arriving on the train where Steven picked her up at the same depot in Abingdon. Susan arrived smelling that wonderful city perfumed odor that all the women in the community came to envy during her brief stay. She had enough luggage for a year's visit but insisted it was 'just a few things' she might need. Steven and Rose had noted Susan always brought more than she could possibly use. Steven thought perhaps this stemmed from her fear of not being 'prepared.' He knew that even after all these years she was still blaming herself for her mother's death and still haunted by the thought she should have done more.

Steven carried the luggage into the house without complaint. And then of course there was the usual boxes of clothes and toys for Randy and many, many beautiful baby things for Caroline.

"Rose, you are looking wonderful," Susan exclaimed when she entered the house. "You are to do nothing but take care of the baby, and I am here to do the cooking and cleaning."

"You're a wonderful sister, Susan. I feel as close to you as though you really were my sister instead of Steven's." Rose told her.

"Sussssh. You'll get me all sentimental and crying. I'm so happy to be here with you. I wouldn't be any other place in the world," Susan assured her.

Susan stayed on for three weeks, taking care of little Randy who was at the precocious stage of getting into mischief. This allowed his mother rest and time to care for Caroline. Randy was still having his meals from his high chair and Rose was at a loss as how to move him to the table with the grown-ups. His dexterity with a fork and spoon were not the greatest and he had trouble keeping his glass of milk from spilling over.

"Would you like for me to work with Randy, to see if he wants

133

to eat at the 'big table' with the grown-ups?" Susan asked.

"Oh, please, do," laughed Rose. "I don't have an idea how to go about that."

"Well, I only have the experience of watching how Momma did it with Will and then younger Rodney." Susan said, without thinking. The mention of Rodney brought instant sorrow to her face which she quickly wiped aside.

The weeks of her leave time were drawing to a close and Susan had not spoken of her sweetheart. Rose did note, however, that Susan watched eagerly for the mail each day and ran to the little mail box by the road. Her footsteps on the way back to the house were slow and her head drooped. But by the time she entered the house, her smile was back in place. Each day it seemed to Rose that it was growing harder and harder for Susan to paste that smile on after she found there was no mail for her. Rose wanted so much to know more and waited, patiently, for Susan to broach the subject. Finally as the visit drew near it's end she couldn't hold her curiosity any longer.

"Do you still see your young man?" Rose tried to keep her voice casual.

"Young man?" Susan asked, obviously startled.

"The one you wrote about," urged Rose.

"Oh, yes, Rose. I still see him whenever he can. He travels a lot you know. I've been wanting to tell you about him. I am just so crazy about him. He is the handsomest man you will ever meet." Susan gushed. Susan seemed very taken with him, but still Rose felt there was something wrong. If Susan had 'been wanting' to talk about him, why had she not done so?

"Where is he from? Is he a Virginia boy?" Rose kept her voice casual. She was pretty sure he wasn't from Virginia or Susan would have said so long ago. But it was a clever way of finding out just what, if anything, Susan did know about him.

"No. He's from the West." Susan stated, offering no more.

"West. You mean like California?" Rose persisted.

"No, I don't think quite that far west. He said Colorado." Susan lied. She really didn't know but didn't want to admit it to Rose.

"Well, what brought him to Philadelphia? Business?" asked Rose.

"I know he is in sales. But I don't really know too much about it. He has to be out of town a lot. So I don't actually go out with him more than maybe two times a month at most. And then he says that he works all day very hard and doesn't want to have to talk about his job after hours. So I just don't ask too many questions about it. I don't really need to know anyway. He is so much fun to be with." Susan spoke almost in one long breath.

"Where do go when you see him? I'll bet there are lots of wonderful things to do in such a big city." Rose asked, she wanted to find out more but not appear to be asking.

"He plans nice surprises for us. Sometimes we take a picnic to the park. He says he is cooped up in buildings all the time and likes to get out. And he has to eat in restaurants all the time, so sometimes I cook for us in my apartment. But Ron, that's his name, Ron, always brings the wine."

"I'm sure he was sorry to see you leave him, even for a few weeks, to be with us," Rose continued. She wouldn't ask about the mail. But she knew in her heart if she were away from Steven for three weeks she would have received several letters by now.

"He said he was going to be very busy. I'm sure the weeks will have flown by for him," Susan's painted smile was firmly set.

"Oh-oh. I think I hear Caroline demanding her dinner. I'll change her and let her nurse," Rose said and was happy to retreat. She didn't know where this relationship of Susan's was headed but she sensed a bit of heartbreak there somewhere.

During her stay, Susan asked to be driven to Abingdon to so some grocery shopping. Steven was still trying to hold Aunt Nora's old car together and continued to take Frances wherever she needed to go. The old car didn't look too reliable, but so far so good so they set off for town. Susan's shopping trip was for items one couldn't grow on a farm; coffee, sugar, and the like, with a stop at the Abingdon Produce Company for some juicy oranges shipped by rail from Florida. Steven couldn't resist this chance to take Susan by the

Abingdon Motor Company to show her the used truck they had on their lot. It might not look like much to others, but Steven knew what having a pickup truck could mean to him on the farm. Aunt Nora's old car had seen it's last. It had gotten so he had to carry several gallons of water along on even a short trip. The old car would overheat and he would have to pull to the side of the road and wait a spell. After a while, he could add some water to the radiator and go again, but that was not a convenient or safe way to travel. He feared one day he would break down completely, maybe with Rose and the children along, and they could be stranded for a long while. Steven knew he might not be able to afford the old truck this year, but there was going to be a truck in front of his house someday, *or some year,* now. That is if his dreams came true and he figured out a way to pay for it.

When the day came for Susan to leave, Rose did not accompany her to the station. But both Steven and Randolph did. When they came back they came to the kitchen where Rose was peeling potatoes, and sat down glumly at the kitchen table.

"I know you miss Susan," Rose offered, "but we'll have her back again. She promised to visit us for a long vacation next summer."

"I'm worried about her. She's too taken in by that sweetheart of hers. And by her own admission, she knows nothing about him," Randolph said bluntly.

"Did she talk more about him? Tell you anything?" Rose asked.

"That's just it. When you try to talk to her she gushes on about how wonderful he is, then if you ask a question it seems to offend her."

"But what has he done that worries you?" Rose asked. She didn't want to admit she feared there was a problem. Susan, for the first time since she and Rose had become so close, had not shared her feelings with her sister-in-law and Rose could feel it.

"Just a gut feeling, I guess," Randolph shrugged and then changed the subject as little Randy rushed over to him, wanting a 'horsey ride' on Randolph's leg.

136

CHAPTER 28

There was little time to worry about Susan's beau, as Randolph's condition grew suddenly worse and he soon found himself confined to bed.

"His lungs are just worn out. It is possible he could have had tuberculosis for a long time, but if he did it was dormant. There is so much we don't know," the doctor explained.

"But we never ask him to work hard. We're much aware of his coughing spells." Steven protested.

"I don't mean that, Steven. The only reason Randolph has seemed to hold his own this long is because he has been here with you. The fresh air and the good country cooking were the best thing in the world for him."

"Does one inherit tuberculosis?" Steven asked.

"No. But a person could inherit a weakness, which would make you more susceptible to a lung disease. In Randolph's case, we need to look at his background. Where has he been for most of his life? First, there was the lumber camp where he would have inhaled lots of sawdust and particles, and this on a daily basis. Then he went from that to a furniture factory in High Point. With the strong glues, the lacquers........those fumes alone are enough to harm the lungs."

"So any of those things could cause this?" Steven asked.

"That's what I'm trying to explain. In my best professional opinion, I am saying that most likely Randolph does not have anything that is contagious, but for the safety and sake of the children, I am recommending that you treat the illness as if it were. It is always best to keep caution on our side."

Randolph was already occupying one of the new upstairs bedrooms in the addition, and now it would be made more comfortable and accommodating as a sick room. When his cough had grown worse, Rose and Randolph had discussed the danger of infecting others should the diagnosis reveal a serious illness. Randolph's dishes were kept separate from the family, Rose dipping them in a pan of boiling water kept on the stove. His linens and clothing were washed separately, and whenever possible were dipped into a large pot placed outside over an open fire to bring the water to the boiling point. His books and other personal belongings were kept out of the reach of the children.

"Rose, would you take a letter to the mailbox for me? I have written to my sweetheart in Carolina." Randolph asked one day, as Rose was carrying in his tray.

"You know I will," she told him and plumped up his pillows.

"When I left, I promised to send for her. In my letters, I've tried to explain we must delay that happening. But now I feel I owe her a full explanation." Randolph said with much sorrow but resignation.

"I understand," was Rose's only answer. She felt a bit of anger that these two people would never have a chance at happiness. Randolph had shared bits of her letters with them and they felt she would have been so good to Randolph. He was such a kind person and deserved happiness. Rose didn't understand why it had to be this way. Had God forsaken Randolph? She couldn't accept the pastor's explanation "*it's God's will.*"

No, she didn't believe God meant to be cruel and punish His children. She couldn't stop the tears falling down her cheeks, a mixture of sadness and frustration. Neither she nor Steven had fully recovered from the horror and shock of Rodney's death, and to think they could...would...be losing Randolph also. Rose mailed the letter the next day and no further words were exchanged concerning it.

It had been several months since Randolph had last contacted the girl he had courted while in Carolina. He hadn't known what to say, how to let her down. He felt his health ebbing away and knew it was unfair to her. He loved her still, but thought it in her best interest to let her forget about him and their plans. He was not even expecting a return letter this time, but once he had read it, he realized he had been practically holding his breath hoping for just this outcome. She was coming to Virginia to see him.

"That's wonderful, Randolph. I'm so happy for you." Rose

couldn't have been more thrilled.   She wanted everyone to be in love and happily married just as she was.

"I want to look my best for her. I have a little money put aside. Could you buy me a few new things? Maybe some of those nice striped pajamas and ah, maybe a new robe with some slippers to match?" Randolph asked nervously. Rose agreed, and hid her smile from him. *Men!* she thought. They are just as vain as women, but don't like to show it.

Randolph asked Steven to help him to the upper porch. He hadn't been out of bed for any length of time in several weeks, and knew he looked pale. He would try to sit in the sunshine a little each day to bring some color to his face.   Steven was not only willing to help but felt this impending visit was the best thing that could have happened for Randolph.   It had given him a reason to fight.   Lately, he had succumbed too much to his illness.   Even the lady's name sounded encouraging; Faith Armstrong.

Steven proudly drove his pickup truck to the train station in Abingdon to meet Faith. The old truck he had looked at lovingly on the lot of the Abingdon Motor Company had actually, at long last, become his own. This was in part due to Randolph insisting that Steven accept part of his inheritance from Papa which he had saved, and Susan sending him a check on his birthday.

"You back to check out 'your' truck again?" the salesman had asked.   Steven had been in so many times to walk around, he and the salesman had become friends.

"No, sir! I believe this time I'm here to buy," Steven had replied, full of pride and determination.

It has taken some dickerin' and dealin' to come to an agreement.   Steven knew there weren't that many potential customers for used trucks in the area right now, and he knew he needed to get the truck down to the very lowest offer the dealership would accept. So he held his own and the dealer made him a good deal. Steven had driven his old truck home with pride. The dings and dents mattered not at all. The holes in the upholstery mattered not at all. This old bucket of bolts was his.   He and Rose, with the children in between, had driven all around Meadowview, hoping to be seen by some of the locals. Steven was proud of his vehicle and was not ashamed of it or of wanting to show it off. After all these years, he had his own truck. He laughed to himself as he remembered that day.

He arrived at the station and found a parking spot. He walked toward the incoming passenger area. While he was waiting for Faith's arrival he spotted an old friend.

"Joe!" Steven yelled. The two men walked hurriedly toward each other. "It's been too long old friend. Where have you been keeping yourself?" The two men threw their arms around each other, as comrades, those who have been through much together and ignored any curious glances.

"I been around. I know you 'member my boy, Joe Jr. Don't guess the two of you seen much of one another lately." Joe said.

"I will never forget Joe Jr.," Steven laughed. "Just as I will never forget that awful ride in the wagon to get to the bus station." Joe Jr. was just a lad when he had driven Steven in the old wagon, but he was a full grown man now. He looked a lot like his father, but with a more determined jut of the chin. He was about two inches taller than his father, muscular and definitely fit for any job. He wore his hair cut very short and had the straight upright posture of a dignified man. Joe Sr. was clearly very proud of this son of his, and the pride was deserving.

"I don't believe I will ever forget that either," Joe Jr. replied, laughing. "Taking the wagon into town with a runaway white boy in the back wasn't my idea of where I wanted to be about that time." He shook Steven's outstretched hand. "It's good to see you."

"And you, too, both of you. What brings you to the station? Not another runaway I hope." Steven spoke in jest, still thinking on that terrible night when Joe had helped him escape from he knew not what.

"I'm seeing Joe Jr. off on the incoming train. He's decided to join the Army."

"Is that right?"

"Yes," Joe Jr. chose to answer for himself. "I've read some good things about the Army. There's a special unit in Alabama. It's just for Negroes, and they are trying to get a special squadron to-

140

gether. I want to be a part of it."

"I've read about that too. I wondered if there'd ever come a day when all the services will be joined, both colored and white, but I guess that's too much to expect," Steven said.

"I know. It'd be a good thing if we knew everyone would be treated equal, but we don't have that guarantee. For right now, I'm interested in the program they been talkin' about of a special squadron to be trained. There's talk about a special Tuskegee Squadron. Pilots. I'm not hoping to become a pilot, but I've always been good with my hands. I can take it apart and put it back better than new. I just hope for a career as a mechanic with the new squadron. That's what I'm aimin' for." Joe Jr. spoke with much enthusiasm.

"We hope it will come to pass," Joe Sr. chimed in. "There's white folks out there that don't think a colored boy can be a pilot. I hope they prove them wrong and the squadron happens."

"I hope so too, Joe. And Joe, Jr. I know you can do it. You've got a good reputation around here as being able to work on anything that hums. Follow your dreams, and I wish the very best for you. I believe in you." Steven told him. "I'll be watching the news for this new squadron. Best of luck to the Tuskegee pilots."

"Thank you. You've given me even more hope." Joe Jr. replied.

The train was pulling in so the three men said goodbye. Steven asked Joe to please keep in touch and let him know of the younger Joe's success. Within a few minutes the train had pulled into the station and Faith stepped down from the Pullman car.

There was a hint of glamour about Faith, but just a bit. More a look of pure country air. She had long hair, which was parted in the middle, and hung down her shoulders in soft curls. She was tall, and well proportioned. Her eyes were the deepest of blues, her cheekbones high, with a slender nose. Steven recognized her from Randolph's description and went over to welcome her. After securing her luggage, he helped her into the truck and they began their trip home.

They talked briefly about her trip up from the Carolinas and about the weather and she politely asked about the crops. They skirted around talking of Randolph's condition.

"I think we need to talk," Steven said. "we're about five minutes from the house, and this is the best time to say it." He paused and Faith waited patiently for him to go on. "You will not find Randolph as you remember him. Oh, the same old sense of humor is there, but I'm referring to his physical condition. He has lost a lot of weight and he tires very easily."

"Yes, I talked with my own doctor in High Point about lung diseases. I wanted to know what I might be facing," she replied quietly.

"That's so good, Faith. It makes me happy to hear that. Then you do know what the outcome might be, and yet you loved Randolph enough to make this trip. I'm very grateful to you."

"I do love him very much, you know. And if the worse should happen, I want to be a part of those last days," she said.

"I don't think that will be in the immediate future, but it is inevitable."

"I know," was all she said.

When they reached the house they saw Rose with Randy and Caroline waiting to greet them on the wide front porch, but above on the smaller porch a very nervous and smiling ear-to-ear Randolph awaited them. Faith ran toward the house, her eyes never leaving him until she was out of his sight. She carried with her a small package wrapped in white tissue paper.

"I'm Rose, Steven's wife. And these are our children, Randy, and the baby is Caroline. We will have lots of time to talk and visit later. Why don't I take you on up to see Randolph now? He couldn't eat a bite of his lunch he was so nervous and anxious for you to arrive."

The two women rushed up the steps, leaving Steven to carry Faith's luggage into what would be used as a guest room. Rose opened the screen leading to the little upper porch and then discreetly left the two alone.

"Fay....." Randolph said, using his pet name for her. The couple embraced for what seemed a very long time. When they could tear themselves apart, Faith tried to put Randolph at ease.

142

"You look so good, Randolph. I had feared the worse, but you look so tan." Both of them were feeling a bit tearful but on the other hand, very, very happy.

"I feel better than I have felt in some weeks. I think the thought of seeing you has given me new strength," he said and meant every word of it.

"I've brought you a present," Faith told him.

"Oh no. I didn't even think of that. I should've had Rose pick out something for you," he said. He was cursing himself for his oversight.

He unwrapped the gift and found it to be a most pleasing picture, a very artful collage of flowers.

"I have a friend who is an artist. He made this for me to bring to you. I want you to hang this in your room. If it's cloudy out, it will always be sunny and full of flowers inside for you and whenever you are lonely, look at it and think of me." Faith told him.

"It's beautiful. I will keep it near me always. And thank your friend for making it." Randolph was clearly touched. It was an exquisite work of art and he would have no problem with remembering his dear Faith whenever his eyes beheld it.

It was a wonderful afternoon, with the two holding hands and staring into each other's eyes. They talked of everything; of High Point days, the old movies they had seen, the old friends who had asked to be remembered. Faith asked about the farm, the church, the neighbors; she wanted to know all facets of Randolph's life in Virginia. But mostly she just wanted to sit here beside him, to listen to him talk and hear his laughter, to see the way his eyes crinkled at the corners when he was deep in thought, the way his smile would spread wide across his face when he was amused. She just wanted to be near the man she loved.

Most evenings, Faith would carry Randolph's tray up to his room or out on the upper porch if the evening was warm. She would return with a tray of her own and they would dine together. Steven had brought up the battery radio and they would listen to music from far away places like Nashville, Tennessee or Akron, Ohio.

The visit ended much too soon with Faith needing to return

143

to work. She had gotten a two week leave of absence, but with so many still unemployed she didn't dare jeopardize her job. And so she left as scheduled, with tears from Rose and Randy, who had come to love her too.

"Randolph has improved so much since you have been here. I hate so to see you leave," Rose told her.

"You don't know how much I hate to go. But I must. I will come back again at Christmas if you will have me."

"We wouldn't want to think of Christmas without you. And hopefully Susan will be with us too.   I know the two of you will be friends. You are a lot alike." Rose assured her.

Randolph was beside himself on the day she left. But he had renewed strength, he could feel it. It wouldn't be long until Christmas, and he would be here, waiting. He was sure of it. And this time he would not forget to have a special gift waiting for Faith.

CHAPTER 29

Susan walked down the busy city sidewalk at a leisurely pace. She loved Philadelphia and now felt at home here. Ron was currently out of town, but would be returning home later in the evening; around eight-ish he had told her when he left last time. He planned to come by her apartment and she would surprise him with a special dinner and gifts. With some time on her hands she thought she would buy some special clothes for the man she considered her fiancée. Of course, Ron had not *officially* proposed to Susan, but she felt certain this was just an oversight. They had been 'going out' for a long while now.....not often of course. Ron's job kept him away so much of the time. But whenever he could, he would see her. She had wanted to buy him something special to celebrate his new promotion, and today she would take care of that while she waited for him to get back into town.

"Great news, sweetheart," he told her just four weeks ago. "That new sales territory I've been hoping for.....well, it's finally opened and they're looking at me."

"Oh, Ron, that's wonderful. I'm so proud of you," she had said with feeling. And she was happy for him but knew the promotion could mean his moving many miles away. All the way to Michigan. "When will you know for sure?" she asked.

"Why? Don't you think I'll get the job?" his smile had turned quickly to a scowl.

"Of course I do darling, you just said they were 'looking' at you. I didn't know when they would get around to making it official." Susan vowed to be more careful. Ron got upset so easily.

When Susan saw Ron on the week following the sales meeting date, he seemed very depressed and absent minded. Susan thought the situation through very carefully before mentioning the promotion.

"Did you have your sales meeting?" she asked quietly, hoping it wasn't the wrong thing to ask.

145

"Yes, if you're wondering about the promotion, they didn't announce yet," he answered.

"Was it talked about at all?"

"Yes, but it looks as if I'm out," he said sadly.

"I'm sure you are the best one for the job, Ron......"

"Yes, yes, but that's not it. They want someone who is a junior partner. That means buying into the firm. And I can't do that." His voice drifted lower and lower. These last words were barely audible.

"What do you mean?"

"It really just means you are one of the stock holders in the company. I don't own any stock right now. Of course, I had planned to buy stock heavily when I became a manager, they get special stock options. But I don't own any right now."

"But you must make very good money. You wear expensive suits, drive a very expensive car. Can't you buy some of the stock now?"

"That's just it, Susan. I do wear expensive clothes because that is the image the company demands that I present. It doesn't leave a lot for saving," he explained.

"How many shares would they expect you to own? And what do they cost?" she asked.

The number he stated and at the price he quoted astonished Susan. But then, her field was more in line with hospitals and medical procedures, and she knew nothing of buying into a firm.

"So you can see the promotion is out for me. There's no way I can come up with that kind of money. So I guess you will just have to say goodbye to our thoughts of the two of us living in Michigan," he said sadly.

That was the closest he had come to telling her outright that they would spend their lives together. The suggestion that they would be going to Michigan together was all she needed. She was at the bank first thing the next morning.

"Susan, are you sure you want to close out your account just now? All of it?" The banker knew Susan well, his own mother being a long time patient on the floor at the hospital where Susan

146

worked.

"Oh, yes," replied Susan. She was beaming with happiness but didn't dare tell this man what she planned to do with the money. But even with the withdrawal, she was several thousand short her goal. If Ron's company required stock ownership to become a junior partner she was sure they wouldn't settle for part. She'd have to come up with the rest of the money somehow. She just didn't know how she would manage it. And then she remembered her life insurance. Of course, she could borrow against that. It was manageable after all.

Ron protested vehemently that he could not take her money. Certainly, he wouldn't dream of taking it with no way to give her any promise of a return on her money, he had said. The stock was reliable, but who can say? Things happen without warning. She quieted his protests and assured him, come what may, it was an investment in their future and she was willing to take the chance. No papers were to be signed. It was a give of love. Only then did Ron give in and accept the cash.

Ron had kissed her finger tips that day, and pledged his eternal love. Susan had mentally started making plans for the move to Michigan. She had even relented and told her co-workers and the other nurses about her impending marriage and that she would be leaving Philadelphia. She didn't tell them any personal issues, such as the money, nor did she discuss Ron in detail. She merely said they were going to meet the man of her dreams, and she wanted them to be present at her wedding.

Susan continued her shopping and picked out an expensive tie to accompany the rest of his attire. Her arms were already laden with packages, but on a whim she entered a florist shop and selected a small vase of flowers for the table. She would have these on the dining table tonight with a chilled bottle of wine. Then she would give him all the finery she had purchased for his initial trip to Michigan to meet with his new staff.

The florist shop was next door to a lovely tearoom where Ron had taken her on one of their first dates. It brought back a flood of pleasant memories for her. She still had time to spare, she'd just pop in for a quick salad and a cup of tea.

"A table for one, please," she told the hostess.

"One moment, madam, I'll see if we have a table available."

The hostess returned shortly and asked if Susan would mind waiting for a few minutes. None of the smaller tables were available at once, but the bus boy was preparing one for her. Susan stepped back out of the way and turned to face the entrance.

A handsome couple entered with two young children. Susan's eyes were on the little boy as he was laughing and running about. She glanced at the lady and saw she was dressed in the latest and most expensive fashion; her hair was perfect as if she had just stepped out of a salon. She looked exquisite.

"Ronnie, please stop that," a male voice instructed the young lad.

Susan looked at the man for the first time and realized it was Ron who spoke. The vase holding the flowers dropped from her hands and shattered on the marble floor. All eyes turned to Susan. She was immobile. Her eyes wide, her mouth open, she didn't utter a sound.

The exquisite lady started to step forward to assist this distraught person.

"No," spoke Ron quickly. "Take the children and go into the dining room. I'll see if I can be of help," he said, as he lovingly smiled down at the lady and gently pushed her toward the main entrance to the dining area.

The exquisite lady took each child by the hand and walked away, in the direction Ron had asked her to go. She didn't look back. Ron walked over to Susan.

"If you say one word, if you create any kind of a scene to upset my wife, I'll kill you," he uttered through clenched teeth. Then he whirled and followed his wife into the dining room.

Susan didn't say a word. She didn't create a scene. She blindly stumbled out the door of the little tearoom, leaving her many packages scattered about on the floor.

148

CHAPTER 30

The telegram Steven held in his hands was one he read over and over, not believing it's words.

Regret to inform of death Susan Williams...stop...death due to own hand...stop...body taken to Bishop Funeral Home...stop...await your instructions...stop. H C Hanson, Coroner...Philadelphia.

They had feared losing Randolph for so long, but his health had shown a remarkable improvement and Steven could breath more easily. And now to lose Susan. Why? She was in good health, had seemed happy, even talking of meeting someone, a 'Mr. Right' she had called him.

"Steven, what's happened?" Rose didn't have to be told there was a problem. The look on Steven's face told her it was bad. She saw the yellow paper he held in his hand and recognized it as a tele-gram. Her first thoughts went to Will in the Navy, or maybe even her own family back in Carolina, although she doubted they would send a telegram. Who? What? The last person she expected it to concern was Susan.

"Why?" Steven kept saying over and over.

"You must go and make arrangements. Maybe the Coroner can tell you more," Rose answered, trying her best to keep her head. She had loved Susan so much her heart was breaking, but she'd try to be strong for Steven and Randolph. They needed her to be strong right now. She would try to hold back her grief for when she was alone.

"I don't know. What could it mean 'by her own hand'?" Steven was still in shock.

"If they think it was by her own hand, then most likely the police would have been involved to ascertain that. If it's true she may have left a note."

"I'll make arrangements to go to Philadelphia at once," he said. "But I don't want Randolph to feel he must take care of the farm. I'll go to see Joe and find out if he's free to take care of things for a few days."

Steven left early on the second day and arrived in Philadelphia in late afternoon. He went directly to the police station. What he found broke his heart.

Tell Steven, Will and Randolph that I love them. The time spent with them at Steven's house were my happiest days. To Rose, Randy and Caroline I send my love.

The note was not signed but there was no mistaking Susan's handwriting. She had her own unique scrawl. No reason was given as to why she went into her bathroom and ran the tub of water. She had carefully removed her clothing and placed them neatly folded in a chair. She climbed into the tub, slit her wrists and sat in the tub while she bled to death. Alone, with no one to hold her and tell her how important she was to their life. Alone, with some sadness so deep she didn't think she could go on. Alone. The police had no reason for the act or any evidence of anything except suicide. Why?

Steven made arrangements for the trip back home. Susan's body would be placed in the freight section on the train. He had argued that he wanted to ride with the casket, but the railroad personnel were adamant that this was against their rules. Steven would have to ride in the passenger section. He hated leaving her alone, but had little choice.

And so Steven brought her body back to Abingdon and stood nearby as he watched them remove the box containing her body from the train. His eyes stung, but not from the smoke from the engine or even a chance cinder in his eye. It was purely from grief and loss and he made no attempt to disguise it.

Some children were playing nearby, waiting with their parents to board the train. They were singing a little song Steven had himself sung in grade school.

The itsy-bitsy spider
Went up the water spout,
Down came the rain
And washed the spider out.

Steven could relate to that spider's woes. The rain seemed to keep coming down in his world too, and just like the spider, no matter how hard he tired, he couldn't seem to get up his own 'water spout.' He had struggled for so long, but the rains wouldn't stop, and he kept going down, time after time. The top was no where in sight as he made arrangements to say goodbye to another he loved.

Rose and Joe were waiting for him at the train station. Joe had asked his wife, Lelia, to look after the children long enough for Rose to leave for a brief while, allowing her to be with Steven to support him at this terrible time. Joe knew Rose was suffering too, and the two needed to be together. Steven was grateful to have her with him. He didn't think he could have faced this moment alone. This depot had seen most of the worse days of his life. Sometimes he wondered what more could possibly happen here.

Rose selected a dress Susan would wear into eternity, Steven leaving that choice to her alone. A suitable casket was picked and floral arrangements chosen to embrace it. A wake was held, many neighbors from surrounding farms coming to say goodbye to the woman they knew as both beautiful and sophisticated. They too had difficulty believing she had taken her own life. They too, asked the question, Why?

Steven wanted to hold time in his hand, but couldn't. The funeral was planned. It must go on.

"We are gathered here today to say farewell to our Sister, Susan Williams……" the pastor began.

How many times would he have to hear those words? The service went on, with prayers and singing, but Steven barely heard any of it. He was remembering his sister whey they were all at home together as children in Greeneville, Tennessee.

"You boys come on in and wash up, Momma says," she'd

151

call out to them. Even as a child, they had looked to her to be the helper, the one who stood by when Momma needed her and took care of the little ones when Papa was sick. Had they placed too heavy a burden on her thin shoulders? Was it their fault she had reached a point of no return? Why had it happened?

Randolph, who had been feeling much better, was nonetheless too weak to attend the funeral. Will had been notified by the Red Cross, but it was decided since the trip from Hawaii would take weeks, it would be best for him to pay his respects when he returned to Virginia at a later date. Steven tried once again to contact Harold, but this time instead of trying to reach him through his last address, had asked the Detroit Police Department to assist in the search. They replied no such person existed within the city limits of Detroit. Steven could hear Harold's words in his ears, *"Once they've got you, they own you. You can't ever leave them."* Steven felt he could possibly have lost his oldest brother forever. He carried the burden of his sister's death alone, except for Rose at his side.

They laid Susan to rest beside Rodney. The flowers sent by loving neighbors were placed jointly on the two graves. It was a sunny day, warm to the skin, but Steven felt only the chill as if a gray cloud had passed overhead.

After dinner Steven told Rose he was going for a drive. He just needed to get out of the house for a while. She understood and offered no objection. Without even thinking he turned the truck in the direction of the cemetery he had just left that afternoon. With only the moonlight to guide him, he walked to the graves of his brother and sister, lying side by side. He sat there for a long while. The sadness consumed him, he couldn't cry, he couldn't curse, he couldn't even be angry. The only emotion left to him was emptiness.

Arriving back home, he walked to the front door, but changed his mind and sat down on one of the porch chairs and rolled a cigarette. He didn't smoke often, but tonight he felt the need. He blew the smoke out and glanced across at the porch swing and remembered Susan from her last visit. She was so small, curled up on the swing, so happy to be there on the farm. He remembered her smile and how her laughter made everyone feel good around her.   They had enjoyed many talks here on the porch on her last visit, and she had left him with the promise she would return for another visit soon. Looking at the swing, moving a little now in the slight breeze, made it all so real…..she would not be coming back.

He thought he could not bear it.

Then he heard the whistle of a train, the nine-thirty Stream-liner coming out of Abingdon, heading north. He had always loved the sound of the train and its whistle blowing at the rail crossings, especially at night when his window was open. It was a soothing sound. But, tonight he was reminded of the trains that took Susan away and the mournful sound touched him in his very soul. Tonight the whistle blew near by, then further up the tracks about a mile, then he heard it enter Meadowview, a little fainter now…..and it was the sound of goodbye.

Suddenly his body shook with great sobs that would not stop, nor did he even try to stop them. He cried for all of them, too many of them. He called their names and cried more.

He got up and entered the house. Rose would be worried.

CHAPTER 31

Steven had disposed of Susan's furniture from her apartment before leaving Philadelphia, and had carried all the papers from her desk back to Virginia with him. A couple of days after the funeral he steeled himself to go through them. He was appalled to find Susan was penniless. She had withdrawn all of her savings a short time before her death. Her remaining life insurance wasn't enough to cover expenses. She had borrowed money against this and only a small amount was payable. He didn't mind that, he would always take care of her, but couldn't imagine what sort of trouble she had been in that required such a large sum of money, everything she had. He felt sure it had something to do with her suicide. The police were unable to shed any light as to why she had needed the money. A thorough search through her papers gave no clue. She had gotten the money in cash, no checks, and where she had taken it and how she disposed of it was anyone's guess.

Out of courtesy, Steven placed an obituary in the Philadelphia paper. He thought if there was a 'Mr. Right' by the first name of Ron, he needed to know Susan was gone. No one came forward.

As time passed the razor sharpness of pain and loss had ebbed, and Steven was left with a dull void. He went about his daily farming tasks with a sadness he knew would ease eventually, just as it had so many years ago with the loss of Papa and then Momma. As he worked, his mind kept going back to the twosome in the Green Springs Church cemetery and then his thoughts would travel to another twosome, miles away at Mount Zion in Greeneville.

Many of Susan's friends had written, nurses with whom she had worked at the Philadelphia hospital. All were in shock; none had a clue as to why she had taken her life so suddenly. *She had been so happy for the last several days prior,* they wrote, *even talked of marriage. We don't know what happened.* No one was aware she needed a huge sum of money and could shed no light as to why. The name 'Ron' was known to them also, but that was all. Steven didn't know where else to turn.   And so the next year passed, the winter holidays came and went without Susan, the summer turned into fall, and the hole in his heart began to heal.

"Rose, we most likely will lose Randolph, too," Steven said sadly one evening when he and Rose were alone. "Christmas isn't too far off. We don't know if it will be our last together. I'd like it to be the best we've ever had."

"Those were my thoughts, too, " she said kissing her husband on the forehead. He had suffered so much. The loss had been hard on her, but she knew it had gone much deeper for Steven. He blamed himself for Rodney's death and now had the extra guilt of wondering why Susan didn't turn to him if she needed a friend. He would have done anything in his power to help; he would forever wonder why she didn't let him know.

"I think we should put up more than one Christmas tree, not just the big one we usually have in the parlor. I was thinking about an outside tree, upstairs on the little porch, where Randolph can see it from his bed." Rose suggested.

"Not in his room?" Steven asked.

"I'm not sure. We all love the smell of fresh cut cedar, but sometimes certain scents cause him to cough. Perhaps outside would be better."

"You are right, as usual.   How did I come to marry such a brilliant woman?" Steven kissed his wife soundly, as if in jest, but meant every word of it.

With the holidays approaching, Rose had taken several trips into both Abingdon and Bristol, searching out those surprises which were bound to please. She shopped carefully and found many items for Santa Claus presentations such as wagons, dolls and carriages for the children as well as gifts for under the tree. Since Rose didn't drive, Steven would take her and most times would accompany her into the stores. But on one such excursion she asked that he wait in the truck. At those times, he assumed she was shopping for him and didn't interfere. He loved the surprises she picked out for him and although he felt a bit selfish in accepting them, her gifts were a thing of pure joy to receive. On this one day, Rose was not shopping for

156

Steven, but purposely neglected to let him in on this. She was shopping for a very special dress to wear for Christmas, and she wanted to make it an 'event' for him. He had not seen her in anything but the plainest of housedresses in such a long time, and she hoped to cause a sparkle to come back in his eyes.

There weren't many shops in Abingdon; she looked at Rice's, Large's and the Parks-Belk stores. After many disappointments, she did find a beautiful red velvet dress, just the thing for a Christmas celebration. She quickly paid for it, a bit too much, but she knew if she hesitated she might change her mind. When they reached the house, she was careful to carry that particular parcel inside and place it out of sight. Putting the dress carefully on a hanger, she hid it in the back of the closet where Steven wouldn't see it.

Steven and Rose searched their land for the perfect cedar trees, one large and one small. With Randy's help and Caroline's excited squeals, they decorated the larger one for the parlor. This is where Santa Claus would secretly enter to leave behind all the special Christmas joy. They hung crepe paper bells and tinsel over the dining table, and lastly decorated the special tree just outside Randolph's room on the little porch. They strung popcorn and cranberries and adorned the tree with circles of each. Saved bird nests were then placed on the branches. Randolph was feeling good on that day, and while propped up in bed offered much advice on just how the decorations should appear on the tree. It was a wonderful time of merriment for all.

Faith kept her promise to return once again for Christmas. She had returned that first year and was so happy to be with the family. Returning again for two weeks in the summer, she had promised the Christmas visit would be her 'annual pilgrimage' as long as Randolph lived. Beyond that she had no plans nor did she wish to dwell on it. Steven and Rose urged her to come saying her presence was definitely a family tradition. And while it went unsaid, it was felt Faith's presence helped to fill the heartbreaking void left by Susan. They all knew it was most likely Randolph's last Christmas.

Faith was delighted when she saw the entire house in decorative splendor. From the front porch which was draped in greenery and red bows, to the upstairs, all was festive. There were so many more decorations than last year, she knew it was their way of giving Randolph his last wonder-filled Christmas. *Enjoy the time we have,* she thought, *there will be time for tears later.* She would not spoil things for Randolph by her sadness.

Randy ran out to meet her when she stepped from the vehicle. Randy was eight now, and had formed a close alliance with Faith. They were the best of chums.

"What's this I hear about you breaking your leg?" was Faith's first question.

"Oh, that was a long time ago. I'm all better now," he answered.

"But you missed out on going to school for awhile, right?"

"Yeah, but it wasn't so bad. Timmy Johnson thought he was going to get to be the pitcher for the softball team. But I didn't let him. I got back to school just in time to pitch. Boy, was he mad," Randy said all in one breath.

"How did it work out, having your lessons at home?" Faith asked.

"Not so good. I thought since I couldn't go to school I could just kinda do nothin'. But my Mom and Dad made me do all sorts of homework and stuff like that. I didn't even get to be just, well, you know, sort of be lazy." Randy whined.

"I'm glad to hear it," Faith laughed. "I was so afraid I would come back and find out you were going to be a grade behind the others. You know, boys like Timmy Johnson," Faith hid her smile at his reaction to this thought.

"Yeah, I guess that would have been bad alright," he said thoughtfully.

The two went into the house and Faith rushed up to Randolph's room. She could barely keep from crying as she saw how much his health had deteriorated during the six months. He was so pale, had lost so much weight. His eyes were sunken and his hands felt cool to the touch. Faith knew time was running out for the one she loved. But her smile never diminished.

"Darling, I'm so happy to see you again. Merry Christmas,"

158

was all she said.

"You look beautiful, Faith. More beautiful than I even remember." He spoke from the heart.

The two enjoyed each other and Faith dutifully filled Randolph in on all that had happened during the months they had been apart. She had written every detail to him, but it was as if he wanted to hear it again in person and she was happy to comply.

It was a few more days until Christmas, and Steven decided it was a good time to take his wife out for the evening. They hadn't done this in several years, not since the children had come. But tonight he felt he owed it to Rose to take her somewhere, away from her duties at home. Faith was here to be with Randolph, and he hoped he could get Lelia to come to the house to watch the children for a few hours.

He wasn't prepared for the beautiful woman who waltzed into the room, wearing her new red dress. Steven was overwhelmed at how beautiful Rose looked. She had taken great care with her hair, and he thought he saw just a bit of color added to her lips. She was dazzling!

"I was expecting my wife," Steven said playfully. "And just who are you, Madame?"

"I'm the woman you are taking to the movies." Rose replied.

"I will be honored to accompany you, Madame. But let's not tell my wife," he continued.

Steven insisted that Rose go upstairs to model her dress for Randolph and Faith while he drove the short distance to bring Lelia to the house. Randolph attempted a whistle when Rose came into the room, turning, as she modeled her new attire. Faith was so thrilled and insisted Rose wear her necklace for the final touch. Rose knew she had made the right choice in buying the dress. She felt like a queen.

They left the house with cheery goodbyes from Randy and Caroline. They were as excited as their parents. Somehow they felt it was a special night and they had not seen their parents so happy since poor Aunt Susan was buried.

"Lelia, you sure you don't mind?" asked Rose.

"Git out of here," she said as she playfully hit Steven on the shoulder. "You know I love these two youngins same if'n they's mine."

And so Steven and Rose happily drove into Abingdon to attend the Zephyr Theater for the evening and to stuff themselves with hot buttered popcorn. The film was one that had been much talked about, *The Doctor Takes a Wife*. The stars were Loretta Young and Ray Milland. Rose thought Miss Young was about the most beautiful woman in the world and while Steven wouldn't have minded a plain old western, Rose was totally absorbed. After the movie, Steven took Rose to the Tru-Blue Café' for coffee and a piece of pie. It was a nice evening and one they would always remember. They returned home feeling like a courting couple again.

Randolph and Faith were still up, sitting in the upstairs bedroom with a fire going in the fireplace. All seemed right with the world and death was pushed from their thoughts.

Christmas Eve followed close behind, and Rose prepared many special treats for the evening. She wanted to fill the table full of foods. She lit the candles, and put on her new red dress again. She dressed the children in their finest Sunday clothes. Steven and Faith carried the frail Randolph downstairs to join the family. Randolph was in his best pajamas and a warm robe. They made a soft bed for him on the settee. He would join the family tonight. This was to be a time of rejoicing, the children listening for the first sounds of sleigh bells to announce the arrival of Santa at which time they needed to rush to bed, and the adults holding on to each precious moment together.

CHAPTER 32

Santa Claus arrived on schedule and when the children awoke they were overjoyed with all their treasures. After allowing ample time for playing with the toys, the gifts under the tree were opened. Randolph had stayed on his settee bed for this one night, and could witness all the many *oohs* and *aahs* first hand.

Faith opened her special gift from Randolph. It was a beautiful gold band. He had described the band he wanted to buy in great detail, but had to rely on Rose to make the actual purchase. Inscribed inside the band were the words *'until the end of time.'* Randolph knew he would never be able to wed Faith, and it was the only way of letting her know his love would last forever. She understood the message and cried as Randolph placed the band on her finger. Her tears were not the only ones.

The holidays went by much too swiftly and after a couple of days into the new year, Faith was due to return to High Point and back to her job. She knew Randolph had rallied a bit during the festive time, but it was also very tiring for him. She was afraid to go. She already knew each visit could be the last, but this time was different.

"If you don't mind......if it's alright........" Faith's voice broke and she couldn't go on.

"What is it, dear?" Rose asked, very concerned.

"I feel his time is almost gone. I don't want to leave him." Faith sobbed.

"We feel that way too, Faith. We understand. And we were so much hoping you wouldn't leave him." Rose held the sobbing Faith and tried to rub her back and whisper soothing words to her. It was all she could do.

Steven worried that the extra Christmas activities had placed too much strain on Randolph's already weaken condition, but the doctor said no. It was Randolph's time. He urged Steven to be thankful Randolph had enjoyed those happy times at the last. How would it feel, he asked him, if you were very sick and alone without family? The words meant to make Steven feel better, instead jolted him anew. His mother, he thought. Poor Susan had been tormented all her life with their mother's suffering. Momma had died alone, except for Susan, and spent her nights and days walking the floor and crying for her children. Steven could only hope his mother had known she was loved.

Knowing the end was near, Rose took the children in to see their Uncle Randolph. Faith and Rose had dressed him in his new pajamas, a Christmas gift, and Steven had shaved him. They combed his hair back and propped him up on the pillows. Rose didn't tell the children it might be their last visit, but seeing the frail hand reaching out to touch them they seemed to sense something was going to happen. They spoke very quietly and were on their best behavior.

"I have a brand new box of chocolates here." Randolph told little Caroline. The church had sent him many small gifts to give him comfort. "If it won't spoil your supper, maybe you could have one?"

"Can I have 'free?'" Caroline asked, being a chocolate lover and thinking one piece not quite sufficient. This brought a happy smile to Randolph's face. The happy smile didn't spread quite as wide across his face nor did his eyes crinkled at the corners as in his healthier days, but the smile was good to see.

"Of course you can have three," he told her.

While Rose had carried Caroline in to see her Uncle Randolph, Randy being a bit older had walked up to the bedside and nervously fingered the quilt. Randolph patted Randy on the head and tried to put him at ease.

"Randy, I been thinking," Randolph started. He went into a slight coughing spell as they waited patiently for it to end. "I got this pocket knife and I've been wondering what to do with it. It's a real special knife." Again the coughing started but only for a short span.

"A pocket knife?" Randy reminded him when the coughing had stopped.

"Yes, and it's been there just rusting in the drawer. Somebody ought to have that knife. It's the best whittling knife I ever had.

162

I was wondering if you could help me find a lad who could use a good pocket knife?" Randolph asked.

Randy's face dropped. He had hoped the knife was going to be for him.

"Well, wait just a minute," Randolph said. "Maybe you'd be willing to take the knife off my hands. That is, unless you already got too many of your own."

"I ain't....I mean I don't got a knife." Randy told him.

"Then if you'll get your Momma to look in that top drawer, on the left hand side, you got a knife now." With that Randolph fell back onto his pillow. Even this short visit and conversation had left him spent. Rose helped Randy find his knife.

Randy rushed back to the bedside with many excited thanks. Randolph patted him on the head once again, too weak to speak. Rose told the children it was time to leave. They would visit Uncle Randolph again but right now he needed to rest.

Faith moved a cot into Randolph's room. He had trouble sleeping at night and sometimes the coughing spells would leave him breathless. She wanted to be near.

Steven on the other hand, was finding it harder and harder to enter Randolph's room. He knew the end was near, and also knew he could not face it. He would not accept another death. Not yet.

The little cedar Christmas tree on Randolph's porch had dried out so Steven removed it, but Faith kept all the popcorn and cran-berry strings and hung them from the banisters. The birds came to peck at the food offered during this winter season. It was a source of pleasure for Randolph to watch the many varieties of birds coming to visit. He especially liked to see the red cardinals and was happy the pesky blue jays had not found this gift of nourishment.

Steven sat with him one afternoon as they watched the birds flitter in and away. It was a quiet time, without talk. The two had come a long way together. Talk wasn't necessary. Randolph drifted off to sleep and Steven quietly tip-toed away.

"Fay....." Randolph called to her one evening a few days later. "You recall the picture you brought to me on your first visit?" He gestured to the picture, hung directly in his line of vision on the

163

opposite wall.

"Of course, darling," she replied. His voice did not sound any different or weaker than usual.

"I've looked at that picture so many times. I remember your words to me, *'if it's cloudy out, it will always be sunny and full of flowers inside for you and whenever you are lonely, look at it and think of me."*

"I can't believe you remember those words. But that is how I felt." Faith assured him.

"I do look at the picture, Fay. And I do think of you. And I think that when I leave this world, I will go to a place like that. It is sunny, and the flowers are beautiful. And when I look at the flowers, I will see you." It was a long and sad speech for Randolph and sent him into another coughing spell. But when he was quieted, Faith relived his words in her mind. She got a wash cloth and wrung it out in cold water and placed it on his forehead. She watched over him until he had fallen asleep and then retired to her own cot for the night.

Next morning, Faith arose and went to the kitchen to prepare his tray. When she entered the room she found him still sleeping. She touched his shoulder to rouse him. And then she knew.

"I should have sat with him. I shouldn't have gone to sleep like that, thinking he was only sleeping too." Faith cried.

"No. Randolph was very proud. He has been extremely ill these last few days, and it grieved him to see us upset. If he could have one wish, it would have been to go peacefully, in his sleep. And we can be thankful that was the way the end came." Steven spoke the words to try to give comfort to Faith, but inside he felt only a terrible numbness.

We will always have our family," his mother had told him so many years ago, *"even though we may be apart. Family and love for one another are the most important things we have."* Steven's family was going away, one by one. All he had left was the memory of their love.

Once again Steven and Rose had friends gathering, bringing food and their condolences. Faith was with them, but there was no

164

other immediate family left except for Will and the Red Cross would notify him. Randolph would join his siblings at the Green Springs Baptist Church.

When they returned home, they felt drawn to his room, the room where Randolph had spent his last many days.

"Do you know where Randolph is now?" Faith asked, twisting the band Randolph had given her around and around on her finger.

They were shocked by her question.

"He's *'where it will always be sunny and full of flowers...'* that was his promise to me," she told them.

CHAPTER 33

It would be several months before Steven could walk into Randolph's old room without feeling the loss, even though Rose did her best to make it appear a cheery guest room. Faith returned to High Point after the funeral to resume her old job and she and Rose corresponded regularly. This room would not be used by the family just now, but someday Steven hoped this feeling would diminish.

Rose found she was pregnant and they threw themselves into the preparation for the coming baby. They wanted to honor both Susan and Randolph's memory with the new one, but Steven wasn't sure how. Rose would think of something, Steven was sure of it.

The baby was born in late September, a robust little girl with dark hair. Rose named her Susan Fay. They were sure Susan and Randolph would approve.

The farm was prospering and Steven was leaning more and more on Joe for his help. Lelia would help with the housework at times. The reports from Joe Jr. were good and he was happy with his work. The rumor they had heard about a Tuskegee Squadron was the truth. A squadron was being formed of all Negro pilots and Joe, Jr. was entrenched with them as a mechanic. His letters home were filled with success and happiness.

"And how is your youngest son?" Rose asked of Lelia.

"Danny? He's a doin' plumb good. He write when he can. And I hears him on the radio most ever' week." Lelia told her with pride.

"I've heard him, too. We listened in especially just to hear him play." Rose told her.

"They be travelin' some. Not always stay in Nashville like they's a doin' when he first joined up wif 'em. But he say he like to meet folks." Lelia was showing her extreme pride in her boys. It wouldn't have mattered to her where Danny played, the only thing that mattered was that he was playing his music. "Some time they do tent revivals."

167

Lelia was at Rose's house, helping with the awesome pile of laundry. At that moment the school bus stopped in front of the house and two hungry youngsters bound up the steps and across the porch. Randy was in third grade now, with Caroline started in a pre-school program. Their youthful chatter awoke little Susan Fay so Rose left Lelia to deal with the hungry older ones while she went to the baby's aid.

"You 'spectin' any folks for Christmas?" Lelia asked when matters were quieter.

"We are very hopeful Will is going to be with us. Faith won't be coming this year, we were sorry to learn." Rose replied. "Will is long overdue for some leave time and he has saved up several weeks of it to be with us."

"That's good. I know Stevie boy will be so happy to see him. Them two's always been close, and now with so many of 'em bein' gone.....well, you know what I mean," Lelia told her.

Rose was regaining her strength after the birth of Susan Fay, but still had Lelia over to help as often as she could. While Lelia watched the children she and Steven went shopping for some Christmas toys. It was nearly time for Thanksgiving, and Rose didn't like leaving things until the last minute. She'd have some additional duties to get ready for Will's lengthy visit. And she wanted that visit to be special.

Thanksgiving Day was a cold blustery one with snow flurries. Steven hurried through his daily chores and rushed back to the house as quickly as he could. The smell of turkey with dressing filled the house. The pumpkin pies were cooling on the kitchen counter top and it took all his resistance not to snitch a piece.

"Who wants to ask the blessing today?" asked Rose.

The hands of both Randy and Caroline went up, so they were each allowed to say what was in their hearts.

"Bless the food." Caroline started since that's what she knew one was supposed to say first. "Bless me and my cat, Dolly," she added.

"Bless the food. I'm thankful for the holiday. I'm thankful for Mommy and Daddy, and will You tell Aunt Susan and Uncle

Randolph we miss them. And Rodney, too." Randy spoke loudly and with meaning. He did not refer to Rodney as 'uncle' since he had not known him in that sense, but knew he was someone his father had loved.

Steven closed their Thanksgiving prayer by asking for guidance and that His watchful eye would protect Will and bring him home soon. Everyone said "Amen."

It was the weekend following the Thanksgiving holiday, the first Sunday in December, when the terrible news came. Susan Fay was sleeping peacefully in her crib, while Randy and Caroline were laboring over their coloring books on the family room floor. The radio was on, they were listening to some "swing" music which had become so popular of late. Suddenly, the music was interrupted by a news announcer.

"............has bombed Pearl Harbor............" Those four words would live on in Steven's head for days to come. Rose had dropped her sewing, as she and Steven kneeled in front of the big radio. It was as though if they could get closer to the radio, they could better understand the words and why such a horrible atrocity had happened.

"............USS Arizona, destroyed.............USS Oklahoma, lost......the air field, nearly 200 planes, lost.........all hands, lost.............." Steven's breath was coming in gasps. He was dizzy, unable to comprehend. Will was on one of those ships. But Will was coming home. No, it can't be happening again. It had happened just that way with Rodney, Rodney was coming home, coming home to Steven. Not again. No, it could not be happening again. Will was supposed to be coming home.

Steven listened to the radio all the rest of that terrible Sunday. President Roosevelt came on the air with his words of condolence for the American people. Steven seldom left the radio, he couldn't sleep, couldn't eat.

No word had come as to Will's fate. Since it happened on a Sunday, the radio newscaster said it was believed many sailors might have been on shore leave. But this didn't give Steven much hope, he really didn't believe one of those would be Will. Will was saving up

169

every day of leave he could so he would have more days to spend with them once he got to Virginia. He wouldn't have wasted a day to just go ashore at a place where he'd been stationed for months. No, Steven was sure Will was on his ship. The ship that was 'lost' according to the radio.

Steven walked the fields, looking out over his corn field, now cut and bare. He walked his tobacco field, with only a few stubs sticking up where the crop had been harvested. He had longed for the day when Will would come home for good, when he retired from the Navy. He and Will would be farmers together. Will could farm Alvira's place if he wanted, or just leave his part leased out, sell, whatever, and stay on here. Steven had brought the livestock Will owned over to his own farm when Alvira died, but he had kept good records for Will when he returned. They would farm together, share the work load together, like they had been planning for all these many years.

It's going to be good to have you here, Steven had written to Will. *It will make the work so much lighter to have you back here beside me. We'll share the load, just like we used to share our lunch pail, remember? I'll help you out at your harvest time, you help out at mine. It'll be great, brother.*

"..........USS Arizona, completely gone, USS Oklahoma, all hands lost........three other ships, sank." Steven heard it over and over again. On the radio, in the newspaper. Even President FDR said it. But Steven still couldn't believe it. The dead were being given in the thousands, *thousands!* They were now giving the number of planes destroyed and the figure was unbelievable. They were saying one hundred and eighty aircraft destroyed. It couldn't be true.

Christmas came and went, but except for the children there was no joy in the house. Steven only went through the motions. The Red Cross was trying to find out some details as to how Will had died, for Steven had now accepted that Will could not be alive. And if possible he wanted his brother's body brought back to Virginia for burial. He would lay Will beside the others.

170

One day a messenger from the depot near Meadowview came to call. He had a telegram in his hand. Steven read the telegram. He placed his hand over his face. A sob shook his body.

"Steven, you must tell me. What does the telegram say?" Rose asked gently.

"The Navy is sending Will home," he said. Overcome with emotion, he walked away. He handed the telegram to Rose and walked toward the fields where he had spent these last days, waiting, praying, and waiting some more for this word.

Steven walked up to the crest of the hill and looked over the acres. They were good fertile acres. He was remembering the days when he first bought the farm. He was remembering his days back with Aunt Nora. He could see Will in his mind, the little boy, his brother. He could see five year old Will, putting on his shoes so quietly and studiously when Papa died. He could see Will, sitting beside him on the floor of the school class room, saying to him *'want one of my ham biscuits?'* And then the grownup Will telling him the navy was a life he had dreamed of for so many years.

There was not much talk of Will during the following weeks. It was as if a spell had come over the household, a spell where everyone was waiting to exhale.

"Steven, are you sure you want to go to the station alone?" Rose was asking. They had waited for what seemed an endless time for this day. Rose knew that Steven was a bundle of nerves and perhaps needed someone steady beside him.

"I'll be fine, Rose. Look after the children. I won't be long," he told her.

Once again, Steven was at the train station in Abingdon. Once again this place was to be a pivotal point in his life. Finally, he saw the train come into view. He waited. The train stopped at last. He was looking down the tracks where most of the freight cars were located.

He watched as the personnel from the train removed a long wooden box covered with the American flag. There were soldiers waiting to take the box, or coffin it was, from the hands of the train employees. The soldier who seemed to be in charge, the one with

171

the stripes, saluted the box with the flag draped over it. The soldiers now carrying the wooden box moved slowly, reverently. They carried it as feeling something, someone, very precious was inside. Their faces were stern, unsmiling, as though defying death.

Steven saw a familiar face just down the tracks a ways.

"Joe, I didn't know today was the day," Steven told him sadly.

"We didn't say much to folks about it. Sort of a private time, you know."

"I understand," Steven told him as he embraced the tearful Lelia.

The soldiers stopped momentarily as Lelia stepped forward to kiss the flag covering the body of her beloved son, Joe Jr.

"I'm so sorry for your loss, Joe," Steven told him. "You know that I felt very close to Joe, Jr. and I know how proud you were of him. I know the pain you are feeling just now."

"I know that you do, Stevie boy. You suffered so many times yourself. If was a terrible, tragic thing that happened. We can only take our comfort in knowin' Joe Jr. was doing a work he loved. But right now, I believe I see somebody who's a waitin' for you. You go on. Lelia and me, we'll manage just fine. We got to see to our boy."

Steven turned and saw the conductors helping a sailor down the steps of the train. He held crutches in one hand while leaning on the support of the conductor. The sailor was in uniform except for one pants leg which was pinned up. The left leg missing from the knee down. The sailor's face and hands were still showing the scars of the time spent in the water while engulfed in flames. But those Williams blue eyes were smiling.

"Will," Steven cried as he rushed to his brother. "Welcome home."

"You don't know how happy I am to be here. Those many weeks in the hospital, I never thought to see Virginia again." Will stopped and stared into his brother's face. He had dreamed of this day for so long, laying in that hospital bed and not knowing what lay in store for him. Will noted a few wrinkles here and there, the unruly hair was a bit thinner than when he last saw his brother, but it was the same ole Steven.

172

Will's crutches dropped to the pavement. The two brothers embraced just like all those years ago when they were children, in the church lobby, when Steven had rediscovered Will with Miss Alvira. They were both blinking hard as their eyes filled. A miracle had happened. Twice.

"Rose is waiting. You ready to go home?" Steven asked at last, his voice breaking.

"Yes, but first I want to go by the Green Springs Church. I have some goodbyes to say. And then I want to go home. For good."

Steven hoisted Will's sea bag to his shoulder and the two brothers walked toward the old truck. Steven walked slowly, knowing Will was still getting accustomed to the crutches.

For some reason, the last verse of the little song Steven had heard before ran though his head again.

The sun came out
And dried up all the rain
And the itsy-bitsy spider
Went up the spout again.

The sun was out. Steven's sun was shining. The sun had dried up all the rain. He was going to make it up that water spout this time. He and that spider, and with Will at their side, they were going to make it. All the way to the top.

EPILOGUE

EPILOGUE

When Steven's car turned into the drive, Rose and the children ran to greet them. Rose didn't know what Will's condition might be, but whatever, they would deal with it. She was just so happy to have him home and to know Steven had his brother once more.

As Will labored to get out of the car, Steven stood by with crutches in hand but resisted the urge to lend too much help. He knew his brother Will well enough to know how independent he could be. Randy and Caroline stared openly at the pants leg, the one pinned up. They had been gently told by their mother that Uncle Will had suffered a great deal in the bombing and had been in the hospital for a long time, but still they were not prepared for the missing appendage.

"Did it hurt bad?" Randy asked.

"Oh, Uncle Will, I'm so sorry," said Caroline and she rushed to hug his one good leg.

"Thanks, little one. And yes, Randy, it hurt. It really hurt."

Steven was glad to see that Will was able to talk openly about his wounds. Will had explained on the way home that his hands had been so severely burned he couldn't feed himself, dress himself, nothing. That was why he had not written. And then finally he had swallowed his pride and asked the Navy to send the wire.

"Will, we've placed a cot for you in the dining room. We didn't know if you would want to try to maneuver the steps up to the guest rooms just yet. I hope that will be all right," Rose told him.

"Absolutely. And I'm to make an appointment at the Veteran's Hospital in Johnson City. They will help me get fitted for a prosthesis………..a leg," he added, when the use of the word didn't seem to register with the family. "It may take a while to learn to walk again. According to the doctors I *will* walk without crutches but there will always be a limp."

"When I think of the alternative, when I think of the days we

177

thought you dead, I believe I can handle helping you learn to walk, brother," Steven told him.

"Rose, we went by to visit the graves before coming home. You and Steven did a wonderful job of selecting the head stones. I want to thank you for that and I'm sorry I wasn't here."

"We know, Will, we know you would have come if you could. And I'm sure you had us in your thoughts."

The subject was changed to more pleasant memories and soon the family was laughing happily as they were seated at dinner. Later, as they cleared the table, Steven pulled Rose aside.

"Joe Jr.'s body was returned home today. I saw Joe and Lelia at the train station when the casket was unloaded. I hate to leave Will on his first night home, but I feel I should go by, even if only for a few minutes," he told her.

"I didn't know. Of course you must go. We'll be fine. I'll get everyone in the parlor and pop some corn. Go."

As Steven drove he was filled with mixed emotions. He was happy to have Will at home but sorrowed so much for his old friend. When he pulled in front of Joe's house, he saw a multitude had gathered. Joe Jr. was a hero of sorts among the Negro population. He had distinguished himself, regardless of the color of his skin. He was respected and held up as an example before their children. The loss of Joe Jr. was felt by many.

"Thank you for comin,' Steven. I know your brother be back today and you needs to be with him," Lelia told him.

"No more than I need to be with you," he replied.

Danny approached Steven and offered his hand. Steven didn't know Danny was home and ignored the hand, instead putting his arms around the young man and pulling him close. After expressing his condolences, Steven returned home.

*****

Days turned into weeks and Will did receive that prosthesis he was promised. And he did learn to walk, but not without many days of dark and deep depression. He hadn't realized it would be so

178

hard. He was losing hope and on the verge of giving up.

"What are you planning to do?" Steven asked him one day.

"When?" was Will's brief reply.

"For the rest of your life."

"I don't get it. What are you talking about?"

"You don't need to go back to the farm. I understand that. The man who's leasing is happy to stay there and it does provide a bit of income for you. But that's not a life."

"My *life* seems to have been taken away," Will replied bitterly, totally out of character for him. "You got any suggestions?"

"For starters, I'd like to remind you our grandfather had only one leg."

"So?"

"He lost it at Vicksburg."

"And I guess by bringing that up, you're trying to tell me something."

"Just that. The man was our grandfather. Look at it this way, to be a grandfather, you have to be a father, which means he had a wife. Now to have a wife, you gotta make a living to support her and the children. Things would have been hard after the Civil War, but this man made a *life* for himself."

"So?"

"So why so down on yourself? You're the same fellow, inside, who went into the Navy. Your physical body was harmed, but what about the real you?"

"And you're going to make some great suggestion that is going to change my life."

"Yes, actually, I am." Steven spoke softly, he didn't want to further antagonize his brother.

"And I guess I have to listen."

"Yes, actually, you do."

"Then I guess you better go ahead and get it out."

"The Navy's offering free schooling, to learn a vocation, a career of your choice. You have earned the right to it. Why not take advantage of it?" Steven asked. He kept his voice casual, not challenging.

179

"And I guess you have something in mind that I'm going to study for? How about ball room dancing? Tight rope walking?"

"I was thinking about when we were back in school together. You had a great fascination for history…..any kind of history. United States, World, heck, even the history of civilization. You'd make a great history teacher. You could teach high school, maybe even college level."

"A college teacher. It takes years to become accredited to teach."

"You going someplace?"

At first the two brothers looked at each other without speaking, and then both broke into peals of laughter. The spell was broken. The good natured Will was back. The next week Steven drove Will to Emory and Henry College to find out what he needed to do to enroll as a Freshman. There would be some courses required to take in preparation for official enrollment, but the admissions office assured them it could be worked out to everyone's satisfaction. The next day Steven drove Will to Bristol to be fitted for a special automobile with hand controls for persons handicapped as he. Things were looking good.

The war raged on in Europe and in the Pacific. The news was full of death and the horrors of war. Steven had been summoned by the draft board, but failed the physical. He hadn't know he had a ruptured ear drum. It had happened when he was very young and he assumed everyone had the same hearing as he. He was classified 4-F, and would not serve. When he received the news he went to his local Air Warden's office and volunteered his services. On the same day he became Chairman for the scrap metal drive for Washington County.

*****

The years went by, the children grew to adulthood. Randy and Caroline finished college, married and moved on to homes of their own. Only Susan Fay, the youngest, lived with her parents. Will was an associate professor at a college in Tennessee, just a few hours drive away, and had an apartment of his own.   He never married, but there were many "possibilities."

Steven and Rose settled into a comfortable life, and weathered the 1950's with Susan Fay as she went through the Elvis and Pat Boone stage of her life. They survived crinoline petticoats, poodle skirts and the hula-hoop.   Now they entered the 60's and felt they were ready to relax and enjoy the wonder of becoming grandparents. And then one day a letter arrived......

Dear Uncle Steven,
You will not know me as I have not known myself that I have relatives in Virginia. I am the daughter of your brother Harold.   My mother passed away last month and knowing she was dying has told me the truth about my father. He and my mother had used an assumed name and I did not know his true name was Williams.   I would like to know more about you. My mother loved my father very much and spoke highly of him. He died before I was born. I would like to correspond with you, if you will allow it.   The letter was signed *Susie Penny.*

At first Steven was in disbelief.   But the daughter was named Susie, and that's a nickname for Susan to be sure. That information anyone could have known and used as a ruse. But the name "Penny" struck a cord. One of their pets as children had been named Penny and the two names used together did seem too much a coincidence. Steven wrote to the young lady, but asked for more information. He wanted to be sure it wasn't some sort of scam.

After a few more communications with Susie, Steven was convinced she was indeed Harold's daughter and wanted to know more. He and Rose invited Susie to visit. Susie had quit her job to help nurse her mother during those last days and had no ties to Detroit. She was on the next plane to the little Tri-Cities Airport just outside Bristol.   Steven waited patiently for the circling plane to land.

"You must be Susie," he said to the only female to exit the plane. The woman looked to be maybe in her late twenties, maybe early thirties, he wasn't that good at guessing a woman's age. She

181

was medium build with lots of brown fly-away hair. Her eyes were dark, her cheekbones high. Steven couldn't really see any resemblance to his brother, but held his opinion for now.

"Yes, and you must be Uncle Steven." The two shook hands but did not embrace.

"This is my youngest daughter, Susan Fay," Steven indicated his daughter, standing by his side.

"Fay. Is that short for Faith by any chance?"

"Yes, it is. But how did you know?" Susan Fay answered.

"Why don't we save all the questions for later, ladies?" Steven interrupted. "I'm sure we all have so much to talk about, and Rose will want to be included too."

Susie had received the picture of Steven he had sent so that she could recognize him, but she was shocked at how well dressed they both were. Somehow she had expected to be going to the country, where people wore bib overalls and straw hats. The automobile they were approaching didn't look like what she expected from a farm vehicle either.

They chatted idly on the way home, and the talk was light, the weather or a current event. Steven wanted to believe this was his niece and prayed her information would prove it.

When they pulled into the drive of a beautiful white house, Susie was again taken aback. She had not expected the house to be so big. There were white columns, long dark green shutters at the windows, and a lovely upper sun deck. Flowers were everywhere. The place was beautiful.

"Welcome to our home," Susan Fay told her sincerely.

"I didn't dream it would be so lovely."

"That's what happens when your wife gets hold of those *Southern Living* magazines," Steven laughed. "We didn't do much fixin' on the place while the children were young, and especially not while they were in college. But afterwards, Rose wanted to brighten it up a bit."

After introductions, Rose led Susie up to what would be her room during her stay and showed her the bathroom where she could freshen up. Dinner would be in about one hour, her hostess told her.

182

"I don't want to rush you, Susie, but you must know we are very anxious to find out anything we can about my brother, Harold. Can you tell us how you found us?" Steven asked her while they enjoyed a tender roast beef and potatoes.

"My mother passed only a matter of weeks ago. I knew nothing of my father's family, especially that the name I had known all of my life was not his. When my mother knew she had only days to live, she told me everything. It was a great shock to me."

"I understand. Please tell your story at your own pace. We want to hear, but we don't want you to feel we are pushing you," Rose assured her.

"My mother told me that my father had, before his death, worked for the racketeers. I suppose today we'd use terms like 'the mob' or 'gangsters' but she referred to them over and over as racketeers. According to my mother's account, my father and mother had met earlier, but when he couldn't provide a home for her, he didn't propose and they drifted apart. Later, he came back and told her he had a job and some money. He could afford to rent an apartment for them and asked her to marry him. There was a stipulation, however. He told her who he was working for and didn't want them to know he had strong ties to anyone. He wanted to keep their relationship a secret."

"But why? That's an unusual request. Did he explain?" Steven wanted to know.

"My mother said that the racketeers would sometimes harm the family members to make their men, they called them 'soldiers,' do what they wanted. And so my mother and father were married under an assumed name. I didn't know until just prior to her death that Penny was not our real name."

"And what do you know of my brother Harold, your father?" Steven prodded.

"My mother said they were married and rented a small walk up flat under their new name. My father had kept his old apartment, the one he had lived in while he was single, so no one in the mob would suspect he had a second address. He still went there many nights so they wouldn't follow him to where he and my mother were

183

living. Sometime during that first year, she told him she was going to have a baby. That baby was me, of course. When she told him that, she said his reply was 'I've got to get out of the rackets. It's no place to raise a family.' He was going to tell them he wanted out," Susie voice broke at remembering her mother's tears when she painfully revealed all of this.

"Take your time, Susie."

"My mother said he never came home again. She walked the streets looking for him, but she didn't dare go to the police for fear he was in some kind of trouble. And then after a few days she heard about a body found floating in the river."

"And that was your father?" Rose asked. She noted tears welling up in Steven's eyes as he pictured the scene.

"Yes. She went to the morgue. She identified the body, but of course she used the name of Harold Penny. She claimed the body and buried him. There is no record of a Harold Williams anywhere. His stone says 'Harold Penny.' And I buried my mother the same way, beside him. I thought she would want me to do that."

"I tried to find my brother through the Police Department. That would explain why no record was found," Steven said, his voice unsteady.

"My mother thought it was safer for us in the beginning, and then later there was no reason to change," Susie explained.

"Do you know why you were named Susie?" Steven asked.

"My name is Susan. I was told I was named for my father's only sister. But my mother always called me 'Susie' so that's the name I use."

"We are delighted you found us, but how in the world did you do it?" Rose asked. She was convinced this young woman was telling the truth and her question was merely one of curiosity, not entrapment.

"My mother gave me an address. It showed a Randolph Williams who lived in a rooming house in High Point, North Carolina. I knew it was a long shot that anyone would still be there after all these years, but I wrote to the address anyway. As it turned out, the lady who had run the rooming house had died several years ago, a Mrs.

184

Stone, but a niece still lived on the property. She remembered Randolph from when she was a little girl, and thought he might have had a brother who lived there too. But more important, she remembered the name of a spinster lady who lived not too far away. She recalled this woman had been in love with Randolph and that she had gone away for a while and returned to tell he had died. A woman named Faith Armstrong. Mrs. Stone's niece took my letter to her and Miss Armstrong wrote me."

"Faith! You know our Faith?" Rose exclaimed in shock.

"Yes ma'am. She was the one who wrote to me and gave me your names and your address. Here, I still have the letter." Susie retrieved her purse and extended the letter for Rose's inspection.

Rose recognized Faith's handwriting. However, it was a bit shaky as if Faith might not have been well.

"We kept in touch for many years after Randolph's death," Rose explained. "Faith always remembered the children's birthdays and sent gifts at Christmas. But as the children grew older we found we hadn't that much to say and later we grew to just exchanging Christmas cards. I haven't had a real letter from her in a long time."

"I don't know much of her except she was very kind to send the letter," Susie told her.

"I will write to Faith at once and thank her for sending you to us." Rose hugged the young Susie. It was apparent Susie was in need of a family to call her own. The revelation by her mother had shocked and confused her. She wasn't sure where she belonged, and Rose was going to show her.

By the time Rose and Faith had exchanged a couple of letters, Rose's intuition told her something was very wrong. Faith had indeed remained single all these years and still held Randolph's memory dear, but she had little to say. Rose was concerned. After several nights of listening to Rose's insistence that they had to go to her, Steven agreed to drive Rose to High Point. It was not an easy trip.

Steven and Rose had attempted it once when the children were young, only to arrive with very sick children from riding over the mountain roads, in a car and clothing that smelled of vomit, and it had been an uneventful visit as most of Rose's sisters had felt she 'abandoned' them.   They had traveled the roads first up through Marion and Wytheville, continuing on to a place called Fort Chiswell where they turned right, leading them to the town of Hillsville. From there they drove on to Fancy Gap, crossing the Blue Ridge Mountains and then down into North Carolina. They had never tried again. But now, with the four-lane highways, the trip was faster and more pleasant. When they entered Faith's humble home, they were glad they came.

"Faith, dear, why didn't you tell us you were so ill?" Rose implored.

"It's not your problem, Rose. I'll be alright," Faith replied weakly.

"Then you won't mind accompanying us back to Virginia, will you?" Rose told her.

"Virginia? I can't possibly."

"You can't possibly refuse." Rose told her.

The day before leaving for home, Rose had told Steven she wanted to go back to her own family to say hello.   Her mother had died several years ago, but she had not been notified until weeks after. And then only as a request for money to help with the expenses. She grieved, and sent the money.   It seems her moving away had angered them, possibly because it had placed the burden of support and work on their shoulders.

At first, Rose had written to her mother regularly, but when her mail went unanswered the letters had grown less frequent. After her mother's death the letters ceased, with Rose sending only an occasional Christmas card to the old address.   She hadn't heard back from anyone in a very long time.

When Steven stopped in front of the house where Rose had spent her earliest years, Rose could not believe the squalor. The place was filthy, with several small children playing in the front yard. There was no grass, only the sandy soil and the children shared their playground with the chickens.

Rose knocked cautiously at the door. A skinny woman answered, a cigarette dangling from her lips.

"I hope I'm not intruding. My name is Rose Williams and I used to live here," Rose began to explain.

"Yeah, I know who you are. You're the high falutin' Rose, one from Virginny," the rude woman said.

"Do I know you?" Rose asked.

"Yeah, I'm your kid sister, Nancy, 'cept ever'body calls me Nance. Fancy car you ridin' in. Guess you got it pretty good, huh?" she said, the cigarette still dangling.

"Not really. We ...." Rose didn't know what to say to this stranger who claimed kinship.

"Momma's gone, you know," Nance said without feeling.

"Yes, I know. I got a letter from my sister, I guess it's *our* sister, Hildred, letting me know." Rose answered.

"Yeah, Hildred. Well, Hildred's gone, too. Not dead, but met up with some no-good and ran off." Nance told her.

"Do you know if our mother ever got my letters?" Rose asked, hopefully.

"Did she get 'em?" Nance's voice rose. "Made us read 'em over and over. Wouldn't shut up 'bout her Rose that took off to Virginny and now she's this rich person with a big ole farm. Bragged til we wanted to puke," Nance told her.

"She was proud?"

"She bragged til we wuz sick 'o hearin' it. Think you's the only youngin' she got. Made us sit down and rite you back, she did. 'Course she didn't know Hildred tore up the letters 'fore they wuz mailed."

"My mother wrote to me, that is, had someone write her words to me?" Rose asked. "And you didn't mail them?"

"Ain't that what I just said?" Nance answered sarcastically. "When she died, them letters of yourn wuz still in her apron pocket. Made Hildred mad, it did."

"And what about you, Nancy?" Rose asked, refusing to use her nickname.

"I've been poorly myself. Ain't able to work. Gov'ment don't help none neither. What's a poor woman like me goin' do? And them youngin' to feed?"

187

Rose was horrified.   She remembered Nancy only as a tiny child, but here she was repeating the same words Rose had heard her lazy father say over and over.   The tendency to expect something without working for it had passed from one generation to another. Rose returned to the car and took several large bills from her purse. She shoved them into her sister's hand and retreated quickly to the haven of the car with Steven.

"Let's go.   Let's go and not look back.   I have a family, but it's not here." They drove back to Faith's home and began preparations for the trip.   Back to a home and a life they loved in Virginia.

Faith's small two bedroom home was to be left to her nephew in Arizona after her death.   And so Steven and Rose notified the nephew they were locking up the house and removing his aunt to come live with them.   The nephew had no objections, he hardly knew his aunt, and said he would see to the house.   Bundling Faith into the back seat of their automobile, the three set out for Virginia and home.

Steven and Rose quickly realized that Faith was extremely ill indeed.   They had not known how near death when they brought her back to Virginia, but they were very happy they had done just that.   Susie was proving to be an invaluable help.   She had experience in nursing her mother but also seemed to need a person to bestow her love upon.   Faith needed her just as badly.

One day, Faith asked her namesake, Susan Fay, if she would walk with her in the shade of the trees on the front lawn.   The fall flowers were beautiful, their fragrance all around them.

"I was very pleased when your parents named you," the older Faith said.   "Fay was the name Randolph used."

"They have told me the story many times.   They speak so highly of you and how much you and my uncle were in love." Susan Fay stopped in horror.   "Oh my, I didn't mean to say anything, I mean, I don't want to upset you or bring back memories that will hurt you."

"No, dear, of course not.   When we have loved someone as I loved Randolph, and as I still love Randolph, we like to speak of them.   It brings their memories closer.   That's what I wanted to talk to you about today."

"Uncle Randolph?"

"Yes. Many years ago, when we both realized we could never marry due to his declining health, he made the sweetest gesture a man could make. It was so sweet and thoughtful and something I have carried with me all these years," Faith told her.

"I've always been told he was special.. What was it he did?"

"This ring. The gold band that I have worn all these years. It binds me to him in love. Inside are very special words. I will never part with the ring, but when I am gone I don't want to carry it to my grave. I would want you to take the ring and keep it"

"I believe this is the sweetest thing anyone has ever done for me," Susan Fay said with feeling.

"I can think of no one whom I would want to have it, except for you," Faith told her.

That would be the last walk around the lawn Faith would take. Her health was deteriorating fast and within a few short weeks, she was dead. Steven and Rose arranged for her burial. The nephew in Arizona was notified, but was unable to come.

Once again the neighbors arrived, bringing food and their condolences. The services for Faith were held in the Green Springs Baptist Church. She was laid to rest beside her beloved Randolph. The flowers were spread over the two graves equally. The headstone had not arrived.

Three days later, Steven returned to the cemetery to see the headstone which Rose had selected. He approved heartily. Beneath the name and dates were inscribed the words "*until the end of time.*"

There was no sadness on this day. The two lovers were where they belonged, side by side. The feeling he felt today was — completeness. Yes, that was it. Completeness. He had his brother Harold's child with him. Will was just a few miles down the road, his own children grown, educated and starting families of their own. Life was good.

The sun came out,

And dried up all the rain.

Steven walked back to his car in thought. I made it, we made it, to the top of the water spout.

189

ABOUT THE AUTHOR...

Doris Musick

Ms. Musick has one other book to her credit, an historical fiction entitled **THE STARCHED APRON,** released in 2005. This first novel is based on true and actual events occurring in Russell County, VA and Pike County KY during the approximate period of 1792 through 1830.   Her second book, **UP THE WATER SPOUT,** brings us to Washington County, VA and specifically to the Abingdon and Meadowview areas but includes portions of Greene County, TN. Her latest novel is fiction; based on stories she has heard from her youth and spans a period from 1918 until 1942.

After many years of residence in a lakeside community known as Brandermill just outside Richmond, VA, Doris Musick and her husband opted for early retirement and a return to the mountains they both love. She now resides in a secluded section of Russell County in a home she shares with husband Larry and a multitude of assorted pets.   Currently *Field Editor* of **COUNTRY** Magazine, her articles appear several times each year.